LOG JAM

MONICA HUGHES

LOG JAM

MONICA HUGHES

Stoddart

Third printing 1996

Stoddart Publishing Co. Limited
34 Lesmill Road
Toronto, Canada
M3B 2T6
Tel. (416) 445-3333
Fax (416) 445-5967

In the United States contact
Stoddart Publishing Co. Limited
85 River Rock Drive, Unit 202
Buffalo New York 14207
Tel. 1-800-805-1083

Canadian Cataloguing in Publication Data

Hughes, Monica, 1925–
Log jam

A GEMINI BOOK
ISBN: 0-7736-7446-2

I. Title.

PS8565.U34L64 1995   JC813'.54   C95-932871-8
PZ7.H84Lo 1995

Cover Design: Tannice Goddard, S.O. Networking
Cover Illustration: Albert Slark

*Stoddart Publishing gratefully acknowledges the support of the
Canada Council, Ontario Ministry of Citizenship, Culture and Recreation,
Ontario Arts Council, and Ontario Publishing Centre in the development
of writing and publishing in Canada.*

Printed and bound in Canada

The journey to reality has three steps: Hunter, Warrior, Man of Knowledge.

Vinson Brown, *Voices of Earth and Sky*

Preface

This story is set in the Alberta foothills of the Rockies. Though the locations are all very real, I have taken a few liberties with time and place. The Brazeau Dam was constructed in the 1960s rather than in the 1970s, as would appear in this story, and the correctional facility nearby is not necessarily Isaac's prison. The truth is in the journeys of Lenora and Isaac.

Many thanks to Pat O'Reilly, my forestry "resource."

MH

1

Friday night and Saturday dawn

It happened between one moment and the next, without Isaac making any conscious decision about it. He had been cutting a notch in the piece of spruce that was to replace a worn-out strut on the footbridge across the creek. He finished notching the wood and rubbed his fingers over its smoothness, smelling the fresh smell of cut spruce. He noticed the white slivers and shavings on the ground among the patches of dry grass and kinnikinnick.

Then the shavings turned pinkish-grey as the sun dipped behind the mountain. Soon it would be time for the work party to walk back across the bridge to the pick-up and head up the highway to the jail. He sucked in the sweet air, which smelled of juniper and sage and sunshine, dreading the thought of barred windows and locked doors.

In that instant of feeling the cut, smelling the wood, and noticing the angle of the sun, he also saw a sudden darkness over to his left. A hole in the sandy river bank, about to be lost among the deeper shadows of the westering sun. Without any conscious thought he dived for it.

It was quite a deep hole, overgrown with brambles. He pushed himself into it, feet first, and crouched, as still as a wild animal. The brambles, which had parted to let his body through, sprang together just in front of his face and shivered, as if in a sudden breeze.

The guard's whistle blew. He saw the shadows of the men in the work party straighten up, come into a bunch, line up. One, two, three, four, five, six, seven. Seven. Silhouetted against the pink sky.

His breath was trapped in his chest like a heavy stone. His heartbeats were deafening. His ears sang. A trickle of dirt ran down the back of his neck. Seven prisoners. Only seven.

He heard a shout. Another whistle. One of the guards scrambled down the creek bank. His bulk blocked the sunlight.

"Isaac! Isaac Manyfeathers!"

The whistle shrilled again.

I could change my mind. I could slide out while his back is turned and climb up the bank, whistling like there's all the time in the world, like I hadn't heard. I could do that.

In that instant, a last ray of light caught the edge of the axe, still held in his clenched right hand. Slowly, very slowly, he moved his hand so that the sun no longer winked on the blade.

Don't give me away, sun, he said to himself. *You're my friend. I'll promise you a…what can I promise you if you'll help me get safe away? I dunno. I'll think of something. Maybe a finger like in the old days. Or a sacred dance.*

He could hear the guards talking together. A rumble of voices, but no words. The men were marched off, across the plain, over the bridge. On the still air he could hear voices and their feet on the bridge. Then the sound of the truck starting up. First gear, second, third, flipping stones from under its tires. Back to the jail. Without him.

He let out his breath slowly. For a while he didn't move. He didn't want to move. The earth behind him felt good. The bramble bush laced a door like a spider's web across the front of his hiding place. Maybe he would stay here till dark.

For a moment he savoured the luxury of freedom. But only for a moment. *They'll be back,* he told himself. *Just as soon as they reach the jail they'll put out the word. There'll be guards, RCMP all over the place. Maybe dogs.*

The thought of dogs brought him scrambling out of his hole. He stood upright, the axe still in his right hand, and shook the sand off his work shirt and pants. He was breathing hard and his eyes darted up and down the creek. Between him and the river was all open country, sandy and dry. The sun had dropped behind the mountains, but it wouldn't be really dark for another couple of hours.

He had to get away from here now. He couldn't wait for the dark to hide his movements. It was three-quarters of an hour's drive up to the prison. So it'd be an hour and a half at least before anyone was back looking for him. Unless they stopped to telephone. They could do that. How important *was* he? A no-account Indian. He'd heard it often enough to start believing it. But they'd never let him escape, would they? Maybe the RCMP were on their way right now...and here he was, stuck out in the open like a single bean in a bowl, ready for them to pick up.

Run, he told his body, thinking about dogs slavering, howling, biting at his heels. He began to run away from the plain, his boots slipping on loose stones, his arms flailing to and fro for balance. In five minutes he was out of breath and the sweat was running down his neck, clammy cold.

No! Stop thinking like a white man and start thinking like a native, he told himself. He forced himself to stop, squatted by a stunted bush, and looked around.

Behind him rocky hills; in front, to left and right, a sandy plain dotted with patches of sage, dry grass, and cactus, and the occasional patch of creeping juniper. Beyond the plain was the river, broad, sand-barred, and fast, with the blue swing bridge linking the Kootenay plains to the north shore. Over there the sandy country stretched in a narrow belt to east and west, its gentle hills broken by groves of aspen or pine. Beyond that again was the highway.

If he was to do this right he had to vanish, like a trout into the shadow of a stone, like smoke on a misty morning. No reports of a running man to be passed on by a fisherman or a crowd of late picnickers, setting the RCMP on his trail. That meant he would have to wait till it was dark before crossing the plain and the bridge.

He went back to the creek, took off his shoes and socks, and waded upstream for a few hundred metres until he was among the trees. He climbed out onto a patch of rock, rubbed his feet as dry as he could, and put his shoes and socks back on. If there *were* search dogs maybe he'd fool them, going through the water. Maybe they'd lose his scent and give up.

Ahead of him the ground rose steeply, its slopes covered mostly with scrubby pine, much of it diseased with ugly clumps of dwarf mistletoe. There was no point in climbing farther. The foothills went on practically forever, right down to Calgary. He wanted to go in the other direction, north to Grandmother's place. But for now all he needed was a resting place.

He found a patch of scrub where he could hide and see right down to the bridge. Not that there was much to see. It was getting dark.

He crouched down, his chin on his knees, and listened to the beating of his heart. After a time it slowed down. He felt the heft of the axe, still in his right hand. He stroked the smooth wood. His eyes shut.

When he opened them again the sky was dark. He could see the Seven Brothers twinkling in front of him. Due north. They showed the way back to his grandmother's country. He could see it as clearly as if it were there in front of him, the little house above the lake. He could feel the stinging cold water where he used to skinny dip, taste the fresh pan-fried fish, and smell the wood smoke. The pain of that loss echoed in the hunger ache in his belly and he squeezed his eyes shut and wrapped his arms around his emptiness.

But I have the axe, he told himself. *Matches I can scrounge.* With the bush full of berries he wouldn't freeze or starve, once he was safely across the river and up the highway. Now was the time to move, while the wilderness slept and there were no eyes watching him, just the friendly stars.

He staggered stiffly to his feet and felt his way down the rocky slope to the plain. There was no moon yet, only starshine, and he couldn't see the bridge any more... Somewhere over to his left, wasn't it? His feet found a beaten track among the creeping juniper and he followed it, his footsteps loud in the silence of the night. In the distance he could see a glow appear and then fade again as the occasional car drove down the highway towards the park, towards the mountains.

He felt grass under his feet. That was better. Quieter. He walked along fast, uneasily aware that he might be going in the wrong direction. He should follow the stars. He should...

He tripped and sprawled headlong, the axe flying out of his hand. He landed face down on something very hard, grazing his outflung hands and bruising his nose.

Oh, jeez. Sticky wetness down his lip. He licked it, salty and bloody tasting. He didn't even have a tissue to staunch the flow. He reached out blindly and pulled up a tuft of grass to wipe his face. There. That was better. It seemed to be stopping.

The axe. Where was the axe? He reached out, still on all fours. His hand grazed a sharp-edged stone, felt something round, then more grass. Hopeless. But he couldn't leave without it. It was his luck, the axe was. It gave him a feeling of power, something he'd missed ever since his mother'd snatched him away from Grandmother and started the muddled years of different rooms, different schools, different "fathers."

Maybe he'd better wait where he was until dawn. Maybe losing the axe was a sign. He found a hollow in the dry grass and curled up in it, tight, like an animal, for warmth and comfort. What was he to do tomorrow? And the next day? He couldn't go on running forever. What a crazy thing to do. Maybe in the morning he'd better just get up to the highway and thumb a ride back to the prison. Give himself up and take whatever was coming to him.

His hands smarted and his nose throbbed painfully. He rolled on his back and stared up at the comforting patterns of the stars. The Seven Brothers and the Fixed Star to the north. Morning Star bright above the hills to the south.

Give me my freedom, Morning Star. Ask your father the sun and your mother the moon to give me my freedom.

As if in answer, a shooting star stroked a line of gold across the sky from the east, from the place of the rising sun. It faded, but as he watched another followed it, and then another. *Thank you, oh sun,* he whispered, and fell asleep.

He woke, as he had told himself to, in the pre-dawn light. He was lying on something cold and hard. His cheek was pressed against its coldness. His whole body was cold. He groped, eyes shut, for a non-existent blanket, for a pillow that must have fallen onto the floor of his cell. Then the memory of his freedom came back to him like a shock wave and he sat up, shivering.

He found he was staring stupidly at a small bunch of flowers. They were bright yellow, blue, and red. Too bright to be real. Plastic flowers out in the bush? They were lying beside a square slab of stone. He blinked and looked again. More flowers, sun-faded, dusty, of the same indestructible plastic. More square stones. A garden of stones and plastic flowers.

He looked down at the stone on which he had been sleeping. Ran his fingers across its surface. Felt a regular pattern on its roughness. Carved letters. He rolled over onto his stomach and peered at the writing.

JESSIE MANYFEATHERS, said the stone, and his heart lurched. His grandmother's name. What was her name doing on a stone in the middle of the Kootenay plains? What kind of sign was that?

BORN DECEMBER 12, 1943. DIED JANUARY 27, 1944. Not his grandmother, then. Not anybody's. Just a little native girl who never made it.

He scrambled to his feet. What was the matter with his mind? It must be the cold, slowing it down. He was in a cemetery. Not a white cemetery, but one that held the bodies of his own people. And he had *slept* there.

He backed away from the grave of Jessie Manyfeathers, who had lived for a bit more than a month forty-some years ago. *Ayee! What have I done?* All the stories his grandmother had told him came back to him. Stories about the spirits of the dead. How they roamed the night paths, uncomfortable without a warm human body to live in, on the lookout for the unsuspecting traveller. And he had slept right in the middle of them.

As his eyes moved uneasily from side to side they caught the dull gleam of the axe blade. It had fallen in a patch of tall grass. If it hadn't been for the light on the blade he'd have missed it. He grabbed it and began running from the grassy plot.

He tried to persuade himself that the spirits had been cared for properly, that they'd had Christian burials and should be as comfortable as if they had had the right native ceremony and gone safely to the Sand Hills.

"It's garbage anyway," he said aloud. "Nobody believes that stuff nowadays. There's television and space ships. There's no room for spirits any more."

But his feet hurried him on. His heart thumped and his head felt light and kind of crazy, as if he were sickening for something.

In a grove of aspen, he pulled himself together. What was he going to do? Over to the west were the Rockies, like a barred door. No point going that way. To the south was Calgary. That was nothing but trouble for him. He didn't want to go back there. He wanted to go east, along the highway. Only if he went east could he get to the low hills and the forest and head north to his grandmother's place. But how? On the north side the hills came down rocky right to the road, like cliffs, and on the south was the steep slope down to the lake.

Once he got back to Grandmother's place, *then* he could begin to think straight. Get rid of the muddle and decide what he was supposed to do with his life.

He stared through the aspens. Where was the bridge? Where was the cemetery he'd run from? He'd gotten turned around, running scared like that, and there were no stars now to show him the way. He listened for the sound of cars on the highway, but he could hear nothing.

In the pre-dawn light he saw a break in the trees and walked towards it. A clearing with an old medicine lodge in the middle, nothing left but a few poles propped together, the rags of long-ago offerings lifting and falling in the chill breeze.

The sun dance...Grandmother's voice clear in his ears. "Our family, we put on the dance one year. From miles around everyone came. A great honour it was. One day when you're a man, Isaac, maybe you..." Then his mother's voice cutting in like a knife. "It's all stupid talk. That stuff don't mean nothing no more. Stop filling the boy's head with rubbish."

As Isaac stared, the sun suddenly rose above the horizon directly in front of him, and in the golden dazzle it seemed to him that the bare poles of the great medicine lodge were covered with green spruce boughs. Fresh lengths of cotton fluttered gaily from the main pole. Was that smoke seeping through the cottonwood logs? Was that the smell of sweet grass and the sacred tobacco?

Isaac walked slowly out of the concealing trees. The long grass brushed his ankles. He passed the tipis, the travois propped against the walls, passed the yapping dogs. He saw people working or sitting by the doors of their tipis, but their faces were in shadow, as in a dream.

As if pulled along by a sacred cord, he walked directly to the medicine lodge and stooped to enter. In the green arbour of freshly cut spruce opposite the entrance the wise men sat silently, unmoving, the sacred pipes in their hands.

Between them and the centre pole the ground had been scraped clean for the altar and marked with the symbols of the sun, the moon, Morning Star, and the falling stars. Upon the altar lay an ember with a plait of sweet grass across it. A single thread of blue smoke wavered up to vanish in the blueness of the sky beyond the poles of the lodge.

"Who are you?" The old man in the centre of the group broke the silence. His voice creaked like dry leather.

"My name is Isaac Manyfeathers."

"Why have you come here?"

"To offer myself to the sun in thanksgiving for my freedom. To ask that my freedom not be taken away. To dance the sun dance." He heard the words come out of his mouth, but they were not the words he normally would have said. He would have laughed. Felt stupid.

"What is freedom, Isaac Manyfeathers?" the creaky voice asked. "What is special about *your* freedom?"

"Freedom? To do what I...no, that's not right...to be able to go where I..."

"Look up."

He saw the bare poles of cottonwood balanced against the centre pole, dark lines crisscrossing the pale blue sky. Like bars.

"Is not this lodge a prison, too?"

"Of course not. I can walk away any time I want."

"Can you?"

He laughed and tried to turn. His face felt like clay. His legs were rooted to the earth. He stared helplessly at the shadowy figures in the arbour. They seemed to be looking back at him, though he couldn't see their faces, not so much as the gleam of an eye.

"I came here of my own will," he said at last. "Freely."

"Did you? Are you sure? Perhaps you also went to the white man's jail of your own free will."

"No!" He tried to shake his head, but his spine was as stiff as his legs. His spine was a tree trunk. His legs were roots. "No, I didn't! It was Ben and the others. They tricked me. I didn't know what they were doing. They just asked me to watch the truck for them."

"They were your friends? You trusted them?"

"Well, sort of…I mean… No, I didn't really, I knew what they were like. But they were the only friends I had. In the city."

"They were your choice? The city was your choice?"

"Yes, I suppose so. Yes, it was." He would have shouted his anger at the old man for trapping him in his own words, his own excuses. But all the strength had seeped out of his body into the ground. His voice was as weak as a baby's.

"Why did you come here? What do you want?"

"For things to be the way they were, I guess."

"You cannot go back. There is no way back."

He felt anger surge through his weakness and the dream figures in the arbour shimmered, became only the shadows of bushes. "Don't go!" he begged and saw their shapes again. "What am I to do?"

"Go forward."

"How? Where?"

"You must ask for help."

"But I do. That's why I'm here, aren't I? To ask for help."

"Then listen to us. You are like a child, turned this way and that by a coloured toy, by a sweetmeat. You are not a man. To become a man you must seek your spirit in the forest. Seek it with a pure heart, and make sure that you do not allow a scrap of food or a drop of water to pass your lips for four days until you find your spirit. Only then may you eat and drink. Since it is the sun whose help you ask, your spirit will come with the sun. You may sleep at night, but not during the day. Follow your heart's way to the river you know. But if you have not found your spirit by then, it may be too late. Maybe you have turned your back too long on the ways of your grandmother."

"It can't be too late! I will do as you say, I promise. I will ask the sun for guidance, and the moon, and Morning Star as well. It must not be too late!" The words tumbled out as Isaac saw himself in a trap of his own making, a trap of every choice in his life being taken too late.

He should have stayed with Grandmother and not let his mom take him away. He should have worked in school instead of goofing off, so maybe he could have got a decent job. He should have stayed with Mom in spite of the men and the fits of temper, and never gone to Calgary...

But all that *had* happened. He *had* chosen, and it was too late to wish it undone. He struggled and found he was free to move again. The distant sound of many voices filled his ears like a great wind, like the heart-beat of the world.

AH-ah-ah-ah. AH-ah-ah-ah.

Now he was dancing around the central pole, dancing around the fixed star in the sky, dancing with his face towards the centre, his eyes lifted up to the sky that shone between the poles of the lodge.

Round and round he danced to the rhythm of the drum and the sigh of the voices. AH-ah-ah-ah. AH-ah-ah-ah. Faster and faster, until the light flickered between the poles and the medicine lodge spun around him like a top. The whole world was spinning like a top.

He stumbled and sprawled headlong. He lay listening to the breath panting in and out of his lungs. AH-ah-ah-ah. AH-ah-ah-ah. He rolled over onto his back. The sky shone blue between the frail poles. The offering flags lifted and fell slowly in the early morning breeze, torn pieces of cloth so worn by wind and faded by sun that the original colours could only be guessed at...

He sat up. The lodge was empty. No elders sat in an arbour on the west side opposite the entrance. There were no spruce boughs forming the lower walls. He looked out between the bare poles at a glade filled with grass, clover, and vetch. There were no fires. No tipis. No people.

He staggered to his feet and stumbled out of the ancient lodge. The sky was clear. The sun was just rising. He put his hands to his spinning head. "It happened. I saw it. I heard the old man. I did. It wasn't a dream, was it? It was *real*."

The glade answered with silence. The aspens around its edge were themselves like the walls of a huge medicine lodge, the centre pole of which must reach up to touch the sky.

He took a deep breath and smelled the scent of wild sage. He walked slowly towards it. There it was. A patch of grey-green in a drift of shingle where grass and wild flowers could not grow. He picked a cluster and then cut two pieces of wood from a poplar and bound them together to make a cross. The sage he tied along the arms.

He held the cross up to the sun. "I will do as you have said." Then he took the offering into the medicine lodge and hung it from the sacred centre pole as high up as he could reach.

He walked away from the lodge no longer weighed down by the dread of his night in the cemetery. He understood that its terror had been an initiation. Without it he would not have been able to see the old wise ones or hear what they had to say to him. Whether it was a dream or real didn't matter any more. The old ones had set his feet on the path he was to take.

He was no longer running away. He was on a quest. Where it would take him he wasn't sure. Whether he came out of the bush alive at the end of it didn't seem important. The only thing that mattered was to follow the way he had been shown and be ready to understand any sign that might be given to him on the way. He no longer had to make choices. The choice had been made.

2

Saturday

Their holiday got off on the wrong foot with a disagreement over what time they should start.

"Up at five," Harry Mathieson boomed. "Away by six. We can get breakfast in Red Deer."

Lenora stared at her new stepfather in horror. The last couple of months, since Mom and Harry married, hadn't been much fun, but this was total torture. *"Five?"*

"Sunrise at six," Harry went on heartily. "Morning's the best part of the day in Alberta, you'll see. We'll get a head start on the lie-abeds."

"Sounds great, Dad," Brian chimed in. Brian was a wimpish seventeen, and Lenora had already decided that she totally loathed him.

"Someone's going to have to wake me or I'll never make it." That was Denis. At fourteen he was really nice-looking, but...well, time would tell if he'd make a decent brother.

She looked despairingly at Mom, and for once Mom was on her side. "Honestly, Harry, I think five is a bit much. This *is* supposed to be a holiday."

"Of course it is, my dear. And the sooner we start on it the better."

"Couldn't we get up at seven and at least have breakfast before we start?"

"I'd really like you to try it my way, Hazel. Just this once. You'll love it. I know you will."

And that was that. *Nobody asks if I'm going to love it,* thought Lenora, hating them all equally. But in the end it didn't matter. She never heard the alarm and fell asleep twice after Mom wakened her. Mom didn't look too good herself at that ghastly hour; she spent twenty minutes doing her hair and trying to make her face look normal while Harry fussed. Then she forgot to pack something Harry had asked her to see to, and that had to be done at the last minute. By then it only seemed sensible to put on the coffee pot and make bacon and eggs.

Harry fumed, but Lenora noticed that he ate everything Mom put in front of him. So did the boys. Then the dishes had to be done and put away, and Mom insisted on a last-minute trip around the house to make sure everything was locked up and turned off, though Harry said he'd already seen to it.

"Just as well I went," Mom said, as she strolled out to the station wagon. She smothered a yawn. "You'd left your radio on full blast, Lenora. Surely at fourteen you're old enough to look after your things."

It was almost ten o'clock when they finally swung out of the driveway. *Saturday, August 11th.* Lenora made a note in her diary. She had started to keep a diary when Mom first married Harry two months ago. It was useful for saying things that she couldn't tell anyone else. It had a lock and she always wore the key on a ribbon around her neck.

Harry drove well, precisely at the speed limit, his hands in the correct position on the wheel. He had thick reddish hair on the backs of his hands. *Repulsive,* thought Lenora. *How* could *Mom love him!*

It was almost noon when they got to the turning for Sylvan Lake and Rocky Mountain House. "What about lunch in Red Deer? I'm starving," suggested Denis. Harry and Brian voted him down. No one asked her or Mom. Mom lit a cigarette. Harry pointedly wound down his window.

They drove west through wide country that went up and down and on and on without getting anywhere particular. The fields were full of ripening grain.

"Look at all that wheat," Lenora said.

Brian told her in a tolerant way that it was barley. "You can tell by the spiky tops."

Lenora sighed and stopped trying to make conversation. Beside her on the back seat, Brian and Denis began one of their interminable trivia games. They had a special car version, using only the cards and some complicated scoring system of their own.

When she and Mom had first come to live with the Mathiesons she had really tried to join in with their games and so on, but after the first few snubs she had sworn that she would never again expose her ignorance to them. The boys had been so smug, and Harry had lectured Mom on the superiority of the Alberta education system. Then Mom had got mad.

They *did* stop at Rocky Mountain House for gas and a pancake lunch, and they were just about to set off again when Harry caught sight of a sign: ROCKY MOUNTAIN HOUSE HISTORICAL SITE.

"Shall we?" he said and turned the car left instead of right. Harry was always talking about democracy in the family, but when it came down to it he was boss.

He was the most orderly person Lenora had ever met; in fact, compared with Dad, he was *strange*. Part of his orderliness came from really believing that other people felt the same way he did about things. It must have made his world very simple and easy. He was always getting surprised by the way Lenora did things — or didn't do them. By Mom, too, come to think of it.

Maybe she'll be able to train him to relax, Lenora thought, but without much hope.

They parked in the neat parking lot, went correctly through the orientation centre, and stared at the models of what would be there when the archaeologists got around to finding it. Then they walked for ages to look at two chimneys and a bit of wall that had been the last trading post. It was getting very hot and Lenora's head began to ache. Brian got out his expensive camera and started fiddling with it.

"I can use this for a class project," he said. So then Denis got out *his* camera and took pictures of the same things.

When they finally got going Lenora's mood was getting worse and worse. Even her first sight of the Rockies didn't give her much of a lift, as Harry gave them all a lecture on the geology of the mountains.

She tried to shut out his voice, boring on and on. The mountains were much bigger and more jagged-looking than she had imagined. They seemed to rear up from the foothills in a very unreal way, as if they were the backdrop for a movie set. She amused herself by imagining the station wagon getting closer and closer, and then suddenly sneaking through a pass and seeing the wooden struts that held up the whole pretence.

The forest that surrounded the highway was, on the other hand, very real and rather menacing. It lay like a greenish-black rug over the rolling land as far as she could see in every direction, right up to the foot of the mountains.

Harry's voice intruded into her thoughts. He was telling Mom exactly how many board feet of timber the forest reserve actually held, and what a crime it was that it wasn't being more aggressively exploited.

Lenora waited for Mom to explode at the word "exploit." Back in Toronto, when they were still living with Dad, their small apartment was always littered with signs saying "Save the Seals" or "Protect our Natural Resources." Stuff like that. Back then, Mom's spare time was always filled with meetings or phone calls planning the meetings that she and Dad were involved in.

So now Lenora waited for Mom to tell Harry exactly what she thought of his idea of cutting down the forests and shipping them, plank by plank, out of the country. *Go on, tell him*, she silently urged. But Mom said nothing at all, just lit another cigarette.

Lenora found herself stumbling to the defence of these dark and alien woods. "It's not fair cutting down all the forests. What about my generation, when there'll be nothing left but scrub?" She sensed Brian's silent amusement and faltered. "Well, anyway, I think we should worry about the future," she muttered.

Harry had been listening tolerantly. "That's why there *are* forest reserves," he now told her. "But the timber holdings in Alberta are so large that it's short-sighted not to take advantage of…"

"Ontario was once practically all timber," she interrupted rudely. "Until they chopped it down."

"Only in the south, where it was necessary to clear the ground for habitation." His voice was patronizingly kind, but Lenora saw that he was gripping the wheel tighter than usual. Beside him, Mom was shaking her head, signalling Lenora to shut up.

Well, why am I defending these stupid forests anyway? The way they crowded together was terrifying, covering every centimetre of land, almost suffocating each other. There were no towns or villages along the highway. No cheery signs saying "This way to Minnetonka Camp." Only now and then, thin and straight as a ruled line, a trail cut through the trees.

"Seismographic lines, or cut lines for fire prevention," Harry told her when she asked what they were for.

She tried to work that out. "Seismo...Earthquakes?"

Brian laughed patronizingly. "Man-made earthquakes, Nora. By listening to the echo after an explosion, oil-exploration teams can find out if they're over an oil-producing formation or not."

Does he know everything? she wondered bitterly. *What a family!* She shut her eyes against the forbidding forest and wished she were back home in comfortable, crowded Toronto, with all her friends, knowing her way around, being part of it all. She wasn't part of anything here. And in three weeks she'd have to face a new school. Ugh!

The boys were back to their trivia game. "Henry the Eighth's fourth wife?" Denis's voice sounded distantly in her ears.

I know that one, she thought sleepily...*Jane Seymour*.

"Anne of Cleves," she heard Brian say. "My turn now."

So I'm wrong again. What's new? She listened to the sound of the engine, kind of muffled by the trees on either side. The surface of the road made a high singing sound against the tires. She dozed and didn't wake up until the car turned suddenly and she heard stones scrunch under their tires. Had they reached the camp at last?

She sat up and looked around. No such luck. They had stopped off the highway at some place that wasn't even a town or anything interesting. There was just a small store with a gas pump, a wire screen door, and a Pepsi sign with the owner's name, and beyond it a few cabins. Why had they stopped?

"Do you want the washroom?" Mom asked.

"No, thanks." Lenora got out and stretched. Beyond the store the road continued and she strolled along it until a heavy wire fence told her to stop. Buildings like temporary classrooms, and a bigger building beyond. They had a sparse, cold look that made her shiver.

She went back to the station wagon. "What's over there?"

"Those buildings? Oh, that's the prison. Better watch out. It's probably packed with mass murderers and rapists and..."

"Don't be such an idiot, Denis," Brian interrupted. "Pay no attention to him, Nora. It's just his age. He'll grow out of it. It's only a medium-security facility. Nothing to worry about. Just a bunch of small-time crooks. They can't be too fierce. They're let out in work gangs to fix up campsites, chop wood, that sort of thing."

He sounds exactly like his father, thought Lenora. *Mr. Know-it-all and Little Sir Echo. And I just wish he'd stop calling me Nora. I just hate it. Nobody ever called me that back home. Oh, how am I ever going to stand a whole week of it, camping in these spooky forests with these two for company?*

Denis really isn't so bad, she decided, looking at him out of the corner of her eye. Denis would be practically human if he'd only stop trying to copy his dad and big brother there. Maybe she should spend her holiday trying to reform Denis. It would be something to do. She tried to think up strategies until Mom finally came out of the washroom and they piled into the station wagon and headed back to the highway.

Why *had* Mom married Harry Mathieson? It wasn't as if life had been so bad after they'd split up with Daddy, apart from missing him. Mom got a terrific job, and quite by chance they had found a neat apartment out near the Beaches. School was okay, and then there were swim meets.

There's another thing, she thought gloomily. Now that they were living in Alberta, she'd probably have to qualify all over again. And what was there to do out here? Back home there were picnics on the island, or they'd go to Harbourfront or the Science Centre and finish up with a movie. Mom and she got on really well. They didn't *need* Harry. And they sure didn't need Brian and Denis.

"Hold on, everyone. This is where we turn onto the forestry trunk road. Strictly second class, so it may be bumpy."

I won't ask why it's called that, Lenora told herself. But Mom rashly did, and they were treated to a history of the Rocky-Clearwater Forest Reserve.

"So do you know why it's called a trunk road, Nora?" Harry asked after what felt like an hour or so of statistics.

"Because of all the tree trunks," she muttered in an I-don't-care voice.

"Original guess, anyway." Harry's laugh was forced. "What do you think, Denis?"

"Trunk...main. It's the main road through the forest reserves."

"But it isn't a main road at all. It's awful," Lenora snapped. *My headache's starting to get worse,* she thought. *Oh, Mom, I just hate you for getting me into this.*

The road was pretty bad. It was bumpy with old frost heaves and hollow with washouts, ribbed with gnarled tree roots and very tricky down in the hollows, where the ground was slippery clay, even though it hadn't rained for at least four days. The road never pointed in the same direction for more than a couple of hundred metres, and it went up and down like a roller coaster.

At one moment they might be labouring to the top of a ridge, and the next they were twisting down a narrow road that fell away to a swamp on one side, while the trees crowded up against the side of the car on the other. The green shadow of the trees reached up to the sky, filled it, and stretched across the little space of the dirt road. It was suddenly much cooler. What were these thin and hungry-looking trees, so different from the fat, comfortable Ontario maples?

She slumped back in her corner so that she was looking up and could see only the tips of the trees silhouetted against grudging patches of blue sky. Flicker, flicker, flicker, went the light. Darn, that was a mistake! She sat up again and shut her eyes against the flickering light and shade; but with her eyes shut, the unexpected lurches of the station wagon were even more noticeable.

I should never have eaten all those pancakes back at Rocky Mountain House, she thought. Now they felt like stones in her stomach. *Denis's fault, daring me.*

She stared resolutely past the heads of Harry and Mom at the road unwinding ahead of them. They were travelling pretty well due north now, with the sun on their left. The shadows of the trees fell across a more open stretch of road, like prison bars. Light, dark. Light, dark.

She could feel the dreaded band of pain begin to squeeze her skull. Tight and loose. Tight and loose. In rhythm with the bars of light on the road. *Oh, no. Another migraine. I shall just die if I get carsick.*

"Are you all right, dear?" Mom peered at her anxiously in the rear-view mirror.

"Fine, Mom," she said between clenched teeth.

"You're looking awfully pale, dear. Are you sure you're all right?" She turned around from the front seat. "Lenora gets migraines," she told the others, just as if she wasn't right there in the back with them, getting greener by the minute.

*Oh, Mom, how could you tell them? You'd never
have done that back home.* She could feel Denis draw
cautiously away from her. For a minute her anger was
stronger than the pain. Then the steel band tightened
and she groaned. She could feel the sweat prickling out
on her forehead.

"I think you'd better stop, Harry."

"I can't stop here, Hazel. If a lumber truck were to
come by..."

"Well, hurry and find a place that's safe."

"There's a clearing ahead." The station wagon shot
downhill, hit a creek bottom, wallowed out, and
climbed the next rise. Harry carefully edged the wagon
off the road to the left and stopped with a lurch.

The lurch was the last straw. Lenora fumbled blindly
with the door handle and felt strong hands warm over
her cold ones, lifting the latch, pushing open the door.
She stumbled out and into the bushes.

Roots caught her ankles and rose canes scratched
her bare calves. She pushed through them, determined
to be out of sight and sound when the inevitable happened. The muscles of her jaw were stiff and her eyes
watered. She groaned and clutched the trunk of a tree.
The bark was harsh, and when she bent over, a spiky
branch caught her across the temple.

Once she recovered she became aware of the mosquitoes. Their high, silvery whine was on the same wave
length as the pain in her head. They settled on her
sweaty forehead and bare arms and legs. She stamped
and brushed furiously as she fought her way through
the undergrowth back to the car.

"Better now, dear?" Mom's sympathetic expression
was tinged with guilt.

Yes, it is your fault, Lenora thought, as she crawled
back to her seat. *You knew I didn't want to go camping.*

I hate camping. So do you. But you made me. "It'll give you a chance to get to know Harry and the boys better."

What a dumb idea. They'll never forget me making an idiot of myself like this. Anyway, I've got the rest of my life to get to know them better. Not that I want to.

Mom passed her a folded handkerchief soaked in 4711 cologne. Lenora lay back with her eyes shut, rubbing the wet handkerchief across her forehead and temples. The clean, orange-like fragrance took her back in memory to the childhood miseries of mumps and chicken pox, flu, and her first bout with migraine, which had happened after a screaming showdown between Mom and poor Daddy.

"How far to the campsite, Harry?"

"About twenty kilometres yet, Hazel."

"Is the road like this all the way?"

"Pretty much. Does she often get these turns?" His voice sounded somehow disapproving, as if headaches were untidy and shouldn't happen in well-regulated families.

"I thought they'd stopped. She hasn't had a single one since the divorce. I thought maybe they were just due to the..you know...the upset." Mom's voice was low, but Lenora could still hear every word.

I hate them talking about me as if I wasn't here. Why don't people understand that when you've got a migraine your sense of hearing is about ten times as good as normal? Even a whisper was like a shout; she could hear every stone scrunch and spin away under their wheels. Her sense of touch was more sensitive than usual, too; she could feel the separate hairs of the plush seat covers prick her bare arms and legs. *I hate plush*, she thought. *Daddy would have hated it, too. This huge car, the whole trip, he'd have thought it was a total horror.*

"You should try bio-feedback." That was Brian's priggish voice, from the other side of Denis. "All you have to do is imagine that your hands are becoming warmer. Then it really happens and the dilated blood vessels relieve the pressure at the base of your brain."

Thanks a lot, doctor, Lenora thought bitterly. *What a pity you don't have a lovely migraine of your own to try out your pet theory on.*

"Shut up, cloth head, and leave her in peace," Denis muttered.

"Who are you calling cloth head, bird brain?"

"Quit shoving. Do you want to go on with trivia, or shall I put the cards away?"

"You're changing the subject, little brother. Okay, let's play."

Brian can't bear to miss any opportunity to show off, thought Lenora.

She was getting drowsy again. Wedged against the arm rest, she dozed, her head flopping over and jerking her awake every few minutes. She could hear the boys' voices amicably squabbling over points, the sound mixed up with the car engine and the tires.

When at last they pulled off the road onto a vacant grassy area with stoves and outhouses, the sun had already dropped out of sight behind the mountains, though the sky was still bright. She climbed stiffly out, shivering as the cool air hit her bare skin.

"I knew you should have worn jeans. I wonder where they are?" Mom looked helplessly around at the chaos of tents, sleeping bags, and duffle bags that the boys were hurling out of the back of the car.

"I'm fine, Mom. Don't *fuss.*"

"Come over here and sit under this tree. It's still warm. And here's a rug. And mosquito repellent."

"Mom, *please* don't fuss."

At first she felt guilty, sitting snugly under a tree while they slaved over the tents; but when she saw how Mom was getting in the way in her effort to help in what was obviously a well-organized three-man show, she stopped worrying about it. In fact, she couldn't help grinning when Mom picked up the mallet and pegs and held them ready for Brian; only she got diverted, so that Brian spent a frantic couple of minutes hunting for them before he saw them clutched in Mom's hands.

He was polite about it, but his face gave him away. *I suppose it's just about as weird for them to have Mom and me suddenly thrust into the middle of their cosy family as it is for us to be part of theirs... I never thought of that before. I really will try and be nicer to them*, she promised herself. *When this headache's gone, I'll start to be nice.*

As soon as the tents were up and the ropes tightened to Harry's satisfaction, and the foam slabs and sleeping bags and all the other stuff was stowed inside, Brian got the stove out and set it up on one of the picnic tables. Once he'd got it lit, Mom absolutely insisted on "doing her bit" by cooking the supper, though she'd never cooked on a Coleman stove before, and Lenora could see that this was something the boys had been looking forward to.

In the end, the hamburgers were as dry and hard as stones and the macaroni and cheese was a solid wodge; the only decent part of the meal was the fresh fruit they'd brought in the cooler. Lenora wasn't hungry, certainly not for hard hamburgers and wodgy macaroni, but she drank cups and cups of tea with a couple of aspirins, and she ate a digestive biscuit.

The others struggled through the meal and then Mom jumped up to fill the big pan with water for washing up. It was obvious that she was going to do her bit on this trip if it killed her.

"That was pretty dire," Brian muttered. "How on earth are we to fix it so she doesn't do any more cooking?"

"You're *not* to upset Hazel," Denis whispered back. "Remember what Dad said. Bear up and I'll think of something tactful."

Lenora's cheeks grew hot. It wasn't fair to poor Mom. She really was a pretty good cook. It was just that the hot fire and the thin aluminum pots and pans had thrown her. Then she had to smile. *Poor Mom, trying so hard to be part of the gang. It was pretty funny, really. And the boys had eaten everything, without a word, even though it had been pretty dire. So had Harry. Good marks for them all.*

Mom arrived back from the pump a bit out of breath and put the big pan on the stove to heat. Then there was an amicable argument over who should do the dishes.

"I've got an idea," Denis said, acting like he'd had the brain wave of the century. "If you insist on doing the dishes, then you should let Brian and me have a stab at the cooking."

"But that's not..."

"You and Nora can do the dishes and Dad can haul water and split wood if we have a fire. How's that for a fair division of labour?"

If I wasn't so sleepy I'd argue that, thought Lenora. *He'll probably grow up to be a politician.*

Then Mom came along, fussing her into her pyjamas. The washroom was a gruesome shack in the bushes and there was only cold water for washing. Lenora crawled into the tent she was to share with Mom. Harry was exiled to the other tent with the boys. *Serves him right,* she thought. There had been a heated discussion about that before they left, but short of buying a third tent there was no alternative.

It's like two camps, she thought, as she crawled into her sleeping bag. *Mom and me together. The other three over there.*

The tent smelled funny, faintly musty, but it had gauze-covered windows on both sides, so it wasn't actually stuffy. With the foam slab under her bag, it wasn't too bad. For just a moment she thought about snakes and got all tense. But she told herself that the tent had a sewn-in floor, and it was really unlikely that a snake would bother finding the door when it had all those thousands of hectares of forest to roam around in.

She woke in the middle of the night. Her arm was outside the sleeping bag and the muscles ached with cold. She rubbed them and snuggled down again. The moon must have risen, because she could see the faint lump that was Mom and the square that was the door. Beyond the door she could see nothing at all. Just blackness.

It was like being in a cell…a convent cell, maybe. Or a prison. She remembered the bleak buildings back down the highway. All those men lying in their cots. Maybe some of them were awake. Longing to be free. She shivered and crawled right inside the bag until she fell asleep again.

3

Saturday

Isaac Manyfeathers stumbled and fell to his knees beside a tiny creek. His face was stiff and when he touched his upper lip he could feel dried blood. He scooped up water and dabbed the lip. His palms stung and his nose throbbed painfully. He was thirsty, too, but, remembering his vision of the old ones, he would not allow himself to swallow any of the cold, sweet water. He only moistened his lips.

When he stood up again his head felt clearer. Something weird had happened to him, but he was better now. There was the bridge. He walked rapidly towards it. Now he could see the river, sand banks like little islands, the main stream ploughing a deep furrow, fast and dangerous-looking.

He ran quickly onto the swinging bridge. It lurched and moved beneath him and the giddiness returned, the sun-dance giddiness. He hung on to the railing and edged along until he reached the far side. Once there, he ran for the undergrowth and crouched in its shelter, his heart thumping.

There was nobody out there. The sun was a gold ball just skimming the horizon. Soon all the campers and tourists would be up and moving, making breakfast. And the prison guards? The RCMP? What about them?

The tires of a car sang along the highway behind him. The sound died away and a bird chirped. Would there be roadblocks? At the park gates maybe? And the other side of the jail? But maybe not. He wasn't a criminal, nothing big. Just a seventeen-year-old native dumb enough to mix with some real crooks.

He took a deep, quieting breath, and stood up slowly. All clear. He ran for an aspen grove. Then across an open stretch of tussocky grass. Through the shelter of another grove. Dead ahead of him was the steep pine-clad slope up to the parking lot. He remembered it from yesterday. That other long-ago world when he was still a prisoner.

"Go north," his dreaming self reminded him, as he scrambled up the slope. "Go back to the river and the lake. Find your spirit and live the way your grandmother taught you." His dreaming self remembered the rhythm of hunting and fishing, of the seasons swinging past as the stars turned. Of the silence. His dreaming self wasn't afraid of mounties or guards. They had nothing to do with *his* world.

The other part of him, the city kid, said, "Don't be a fool. You've done the smart thing, lying low all night. Don't blow it now." He ran over his options again. North was impossible; the hills rose steep and rocky, almost cliffs. He had to take the highway to get out of here: west into the mountains — and there was nothing for him there — or east, and that was towards the jail.

Towards the jail. That was the catch. Once past the lake, the imprisoning rocks to the north drew back and softened into foothills, which were gentle, welcoming; but how was he to get up that stretch of highway? Cliffs on his left. The lake on his right. He hadn't a chance of not being seen.

Now he was level with the road, looking out across

the parking lot from the shadow of a pine. The highway was deserted at the moment, but he knew it wouldn't be for long. Soon the campers would have had their coffee and bacon and eggs — his stomach knotted at the thought of food — and they'd be off on their restless way to the next place. What was he to do?

Clatter, clatter. He shrank close to the comforting tree. Around the curve from the east came an ancient pickup, its transmission whining painfully, its muffler clattering. It stopped with a shudder only a pebble's throw from Isaac's hiding place.

Even before the old man climbed down from the cab, Isaac knew he was one of his own kind. Only a native would drive a disaster of a truck like that, its muffler hanging askew, rust eating in boils and flakes through the faded pink that had long ago been maroon. Only a native would have the kind of faith to make the pickup run, or the patience to repair it when it didn't.

The old man climbed painfully down. His body was thin and twisted, as old and beat-up as the truck. He hobbled into the bush over to Isaac's right. When he returned he sat on a rock in the sun and began to roll a cigarette, slowly, as if he had all day.

Isaac straightened up and walked very quietly towards the parking lot, the axe dragging at the muscles of his right arm. The old man's head was bent over a match. The tip of the homemade cigarette flared and a drift of pungent smoke rose in the still air. Crazy thoughts darted through Isaac's head, jail thoughts.

If he could get hold of the old man's car keys…make him… His heavy work boot dislodged a stone. It rolled along in front of him and was brought to a stop, with a tiny click, against the rock where the old man was sitting.

Isaac stood frozen, discovered in the open, wondering

whether to run, whether to brazen it out. The old man bent down, picked up the stone, and rolled it around in the palm of his hand.

"Buffalo stone. Good luck for you." He held it out.

Isaac drew back. "It's yours, not mine."

"Your foot uncovered it. You take it. Keep it. Buffalo stone'll bring you plenty luck."

Isaac laughed. The noise came out of his dry throat like the voice of an old crow. Four steps brought him to the old man's side. He took the stone from a palm that might have been made of hundred-year-old leather and ran his fingers around the stone's whorls. It was like a huge snail made out of stone. "Luck? I could use it," he muttered.

"Want a lift anywhere?"

He stared down at the old man. Did he know him? Was he...? But his face was in shadow, his hand nursing the cigarette. Maybe this buffalo stone *was* going to bring him luck. He nodded, speechless.

"Where d'you want to go?"

"East and then north." He felt as if he'd been kicked in the stomach by a horse, but he managed to get the words out. He stared down at the buffalo stone, clenched his fingers around it, and put it carefully in his shirt pocket. Lucky? If he hadn't dislodged that stone, he might have killed the old man.

"Through the mountains?"

"No. Into the bush. Up to the Brazeau."

"Want me to drop you off at the forestry road?"

"Not the road. Maybe some trail going the same way. You know any trails I could take would get me there?"

"Maybe. Hop in the back. Under the tarp there. No one'll see you."

Without looking around to see if Isaac was following him, the old man pinched out his cigarette between a gnarled finger and thumb and put the stub into the pocket of his mackinaw. He straightened slowly and ambled over to the cab of the truck. He'd never seen Isaac's face. Isaac had not seen his. But he was like someone sent...

Isaac pulled himself together, ran across the lot to the truck, and jumped over the tailgate. There was the tarp, tied down in front, loose at the back. Under it every kind of garbage. Some smelled okay. Some not so good. He crouched low, his heart thumping. How had the old man known? It was like he'd been waiting for him. Not just a rest and a smoke, but waiting for *him*. The engine coughed, spluttered, and caught. The truck began to turn in a series of short jerks.

It was a bone-shaking ride. The truck had long ago given up on springs, and it didn't seem to have a top gear, either. It groaned up the hills and clattered down into the valleys. Isaac shuffled across the floorboards on his knees until he was against the side of the truck. Now he had something reasonably solid to lean against and, if he lifted the tarp just a bit, fresh air poured in and he could catch an occasional glimpse of where they were.

Blue. That was the lake. Another white man's hand on the land, spoiling what had been there forever. A creek bottom. Two more. Now he could see ahead to the gas station and the gift shop above the Big Horn Reserve. Maybe where the old man had come from. But *how* had he known he was needed?

He saw the RCMP car waiting at the gas pump and ducked just as the truck swerved across the oncoming traffic and turned up a dirt road on the north side of the highway. He was tossed to the floor, bit his tongue, and tasted blood.

The dirt road was one huge pothole. He hung onto the side of the truck with both hands. A lump of something heavy slid out of the garbage and whacked into the backs of his legs. The truck turned left and suddenly stopped.

He poked his head up. It was a quiet tree place. Even above the sound of the engine he could tell that. He climbed down and walked along until he was standing below the cab, his hand on the frame of the door.

"The dump's along this road." He heard the old man's quiet voice. "I'll just drop off this load before I go back. That's what I came here for, if anyone should ask."

"Maybe they saw you driving west, down to the plain. Suppose they ask? What *were* you doing there? How did you *know*?"

"Looking for bottles, that's all." Was the old man smiling? Isaac couldn't see his face clearly. "You go along the road there. Take the turn on the right that leads up to the campgrounds. There's a trail up there, a good trail. It'll take you right up to Brown Creek. Know it?"

He shook his head. "Seen a map once. Not sure now."

He heard the old man sigh. "Hope you know what you're doing. Take the right-hand trail all the way up till you reach the Blackstone River. That's maybe twenty-six miles. Got that?"

"Sure. Right-hand trail all the way."

"At Blackstone the trail goes left and right. You'd best take the left fork. It'll take you around to join a dirt road that circles and then joins the forestry road below Brown Creek. If you forget and take the right fork through Blackstone Gap, it brings you out at a campsite a bit further south. Either way, you finish up on the forestry road. There's no more good trails between the road and the Brazeau."

"Thanks. I'll follow the cut lines after that."

"Know where you're going?"

"I'll know it when I see it. My grandmother's place. She's got a cabin up that way." For a moment he wanted to share with the old man his memory of the sun dance. But it was something that was his alone. The old man was a good friend, lending a hand like this, but…"I need to go back," he said in the end.

"Yeah? Good luck, son. It'll be three, maybe four days' hard walking. What about grub? I've got some stuff here. You're welcome."

Grub. The hungry knot in Isaac's stomach tightened and he swallowed a sudden gush of saliva. It was crazy to go off into the bush, three, four days of walking, with nothing to eat. He'd get sick, maybe die of hunger…

Seek your spirit with a pure heart, he remembered. *Make sure you do not allow a scrap of food or a drop of water to pass your lips until you find your spirit.*

Where had those words come from? Had it really been the old ones speaking? Or just something inside his own head, maybe from Grandmother's stories?

"You're welcome to some grub," the old man repeated as Isaac hesitated.

"No, it's okay. But I'd be glad of some matches, if you could spare them. Thanks, man."

Isaac watched the truck lurch and sway down the side road to the dump. Then he backtracked and began to walk along the dirt road. He came to the fork. *Crescent Falls campground.* He slogged along, ready to dive for the bushes if he heard a car. Now he could smell wood smoke. Coffee and bacon. His stomach muscles knotted and churned again.

The noise of an engine ripped through the air and he rolled into the ditch, down among the fronds of horsetail and the spiky branches of wild rose. Two motorcycles came zipping along the dirt road, the riders black-jacketed, helmeted, bowed down with sleeping bags and rucksacks.

When they had passed he left the road and took to the bush above the camping grounds. The land sloped steeply and the going was slow, but he felt safer away from people. Twenty, thirty paces to his left he glimpsed tents, trailers, a big motor home. He moved quietly from pine to pine until he was past the last site.

A path, brown-carpeted with fallen pine needles, curved up to meet him. He walked briskly along. The smells and sounds of people were swallowed up in the quietness of the forest.

Once or twice his mind's ear heard the whisper of faint pursuit. He stopped, turned quickly, stared through the tree shadows. But there was nothing there. After a time he realized that it wasn't the idea of the mounties following him that scared him. It was those others, the spirits he had disturbed in the cemetery. Was he through with them? Or would they be following him all the way into the forest, day after day...worse...night after night?

Jessie Manyfeathers. She had my grandmother's name. If she's an ancestor of mine she shouldn't bug me. She should be helping me. Maybe it's all right. Maybe she'll keep the others away. He stopped and listened, but all he could hear was the screech of whisky-jacks and the chitter of squirrels. *It's just superstition anyway,* he told himself, and walked on.

Then he stopped. If the cemetery didn't mean anything, then maybe the sun-dance place didn't, either. Maybe he was heading into the bush for nothing. Like a crazy man. If he believed in the one, he was stuck with believing in the other, wasn't he? He gritted his teeth and walked on. He refused to turn around when he thought he heard sounds behind him. After a while, they seemed to go away.

By the time the sun was directly overhead, the trail had led him downhill, across an empty creek, and to the first fork. "Take the right-hand trail all the way up," the old man had said. He turned right. Due north. With the sun between his shoulder blades he set off again. It was getting very warm. He took off his shirt and tied it around his waist.

Now the trail was mostly uphill, but it wasn't too steep. He came to a crest from which he could see down over the ocean of trees. There was a jog and the trail turned west, towards the mountains. *I must trust the old man,* Isaac told himself. *He wouldn't lead me astray. He was a good man. The trail's just going around a difficult bit of land.*

Sure enough, after a while the trail headed north again. The hills closed in on him. He walked up a valley with a small river for company. Now the sun was on his left cheek. It danced on the water. Clean water running over pebbles with a small chuckling sound. He ran his tongue over his lips. They felt cracked and sore. Jeez, he was thirsty!

Once he'd thought of just how thirsty he was, the thought plagued him worse than the flies that rose out of the low bushes and the thick grass. He pushed the thought away and climbed on.

The little river dried up and the trail led along a dry creek bed edged with rough grass and silvery wolf willow. West and northwest the trail wound, towards the mountains. Sometimes he caught a glimpse of tan rock or a gleam of white snow. But mostly he saw just the forest and the clear trail. It was a mindless slog up and down, across the dry creek and back again.

It was evening when he came to a watershed. It was getting cold, he realized, and he stopped to put on his shirt and button it up to the neck. Now there was a new creek, flowing north and east. Another creek joined it, and then another. It became a sizable stream. Was this the Blackstone River?

When he came to the next fork he stopped to think it out. Right or left? It wasn't much of a river. Still just a stream. And the trail didn't really divide left and right the way the old man had said. The right fork headed just about due north. It felt lucky.

But the stop told him just how tired his body was. As soon as he thought about it, he realized that he was practically falling down. His knees trembled. His ankles were floppy. Hunger gnawed at his belly and he couldn't stop shivering. Time to find somewhere to sleep.

He wandered on for a bit, in the hope of finding a better place. In the end he turned off the trail to where a huge spruce stood solitary among lesser spruce and pine. It seemed to welcome him with its outstretched branches. He crawled under it, piled soft needles into a mound to support his neck, and curled up close to the warmth of the trunk.

His legs twitched with fatigue, and inside his head he still seemed to be walking. Memories flashed across his mind...

His last fight with Mom, slamming out of the rooming house with nothing but small change in his pocket, hitching rides down to Calgary, half scared, half believing that he'd get a great job and show her.

Walking the streets, looking at help-wanted signs.

"What kind of education, fella?"

"Grade ten."

"Experience?"

"Uh...dishwasher at Mother Tucker's."

"Yeah?"

"...and bussing tables."

"Sorry. Nothing for you today."

Walking till his feet swelled, feeling the last few coins in his jeans pocket. The single men's hostel with the stink of booze overlaying the sharp smell of disinfectant. The closeness and noise that made his flesh creep. For *this* he'd run away?

Ready to go back to Edmonton when the job at the car wash turned up. Sounded okay. December nights, scrubbing down the wash and the concrete apron, chipping away at the chunks of ice until his hands swelled and cracked. Spending food money on work gloves, cheap ones that split up the sides after a couple of weeks. Hanging in through January. February.

"Have to let you go Saturday. Sorry."

"Haven't I been doing okay?"

"Sure. No complaints. But it's like this, the fella that used to work here, well, he's a friend of the family and he wants his old job back."

"That's not *fair*!"

"Sorry."

Lining up at the unemployment office. "But you've only worked two and a half months..."

"The other guy came back and they let me go."

"Sorry, you don't qualify. Look at the notices on the board over there. Maybe you'll see something."

By spring, with his few savings dwindled to change, scrounging bottles out of trash cans with the rubbies...

"Jeez, you'd be better off on welfare," someone said, and told him where to go. But it was worse than the unemployment office.

"Why don't you go home? Go back to your reserve. They'll look after you there."

Trying to explain about Mom taking him away from Grandmother and about trying to make good on his own, but it was useless.

"We can't begin to process you when you've got no fixed address. Go home. It's the best thing."

Isaac turned over restlessly on the hard ground. Why were people treated like lepers just because they didn't have an address and a regular job? If Grandmother's stories were right, his people had done pretty well for thousands of years with no fixed address. They were meaningless words, anyway. This earth under his back was home. This spruce above his head was home. This forest was his address.

Comforted by the thought, he curled up around the emptiness of his stomach and fell asleep. But later in the night his dreams came back to plague him. His so-called friends, Ben, Jim, and Moses, in a bar, treating him to beer, like real friends. In the dream, their faces grinned like evil spirit masks.

Come on, fella. Join us. Be part of the real world.

Then, in his dream, he was alone and it was dark and he was terribly frightened. There was a blaze of blinding light and cops shouting.

"What's your name?

"Whose truck is this?"

"Where are your friends?"

"What are you doing here?"

I don't know. I don't know. I don't know.

His body jerked and trembled. He groaned and turned over, his fingers digging into the soft brown dirt. Then his hands relaxed and he slept again.

4

Sunday

Lenora opened her eyes and stared sleepily at the pattern of sunshine and shadow on the tent wall. She lifted her head cautiously. *Wow, no more headache! Fantastic.* Sometimes it took two days to get rid of a migraine.

She took a deep breath and sniffed. A woodsy, mysterious smell, overlaid with freshly brewed coffee and cooking bacon. Her stomach growled. It was ages since she'd had a decent meal, yesterday's lunch, in fact. She wriggled into jeans and a fresh shirt. Mom was still a lump in the sleeping bag beside her. She grinned. So the boys had beaten Mom to the cookstove. Well, she wouldn't fight that.

She crawled through the doorway and stood up. It was much earlier than she had thought. The shadows of the pines stretched clear across the campsite. The air had a tang to it, and the bottoms of her jeans got soaked with dew as she trudged through the grass to the outhouse. It was chilly, too. Chilly enough for a sweater.

She was wrapped in the spaced-out calm that followed a migraine attack. Everything looked extra-bright, extra-beautiful. She found herself staring happily at the texture of the fungus on the trees and the detail of cobwebs spun between weeds, each thread strung with minute, pearl-like drops of dew.

She got a sweater and perched on the edge of the picnic table. Denis was turning the bacon in one pan while Brian stirred hash browns in another. They worked together neatly, she noticed, with a minimum of fuss. A team, she thought, with no room for number three. But I must try...

"That smells absolutely terrific."

"You hungry?"

"Mm. *Starving.*"

"Hang on and I'll fry you a couple of eggs." Denis pushed the bacon to the side of the pan and broke two eggs into the hot fat. "And a drop of water. Makes them tender." He covered the pan and poured her a cup of coffee.

She sat with her hands wrapped around the mug while he slid the eggs onto a plastic plate, then added three rashers of bacon, a mound of hash browns, and a sliced tomato. "See how that does."

"Thanks. It looks great." She sat at the far end of the table, where the sun was just beginning to shine. It wasn't really warm yet, but she had the feeling that in a couple of hours it might be a great day for getting a tan.

Brian filled two plates with food and placed them at the opposite end of the table before filling the pans with more bacon and potatoes. They ate in silence until Lenora tried again.

"This is fantastic, Denis. How can you do it on just a two-burner Coleman?"

"Oh, it's just a knack." Denis poured more coffee and sat down next to her, pulling his plate over.

Brian interrupted laughing: "You should have seen little brother a couple of years ago. What a klutz! He couldn't even fry an egg without breaking it."

Lenora decided to ignore him. "I suppose you...could you teach me to cook like this, Denis?"

"There's not much to it, but sure. I'd be glad to. Don't listen to Brian there."

"I don't intend to..."

"There's a kind of tradition in this family," Brian interrupted again, "that the men do the cooking in camp."

"Leaving the women with the greasy dishes? Yes, I heard you working that out last night. I wasn't feeling up to arguing the point then, but I certainly didn't give you my vote. As far as I'm concerned, if you want to hog the cooking you can do the dishes, too. Otherwise it's turnabouts...that is, if Denis doesn't mind teaching me."

Denis looked uneasily from her to Brian. Brian didn't say a thing, just looked back with a sneer and one raised eyebrow.

Even from inside her comfortable cocoon feeling, Lenora felt herself getting angry. She took a deep breath. "Let's be fair, Brian. Family traditions have to be adapted to family changes. Surely you agree?"

She was quite proud of the way she had said that, without losing her cool or stammering or anything. Brian looked surprised, but then acted as if he hadn't heard her and went on shovelling hash browns into his mouth.

Just then Mom crawled out of the tent wearing a fluffy negligee that looked totally wrong for camping. Her hair was a mess and she hadn't done anything to it yet. She started flattering the boys about their cooking. "...I see I'll have to be up at the crack of dawn if I'm to beat you guys to the stove," she joked, and Lenora saw Brian nudge Denis.

Her face flamed and she was about to lose her cool completely when Harry appeared, freshly shaved and as neatly turned out, in clean jeans and a plaid shirt, as if he were going to a square dance. His appearance made Mom look even more bedraggled, and Lenora wished she would stop hovering around in her night things and get her act together.

Harry filled a plate full of food, rubbed his hands together briskly, and set to. "I've found just the spot for fishing, fellas. About a kilometre upstream. Let's get going before the sun heats up the water."

"Ready when you are, Dad," said Denis.

"Just got this coffee to finish, Dad. My gear's all set."

"Gear? Oh dear, I don't have any fishing stuff. Can I borrow...?" Lenora began eagerly. Her voice faded as Brian looked meaningfully at Harry, and Harry looked at Mom.

"I think it would be a good idea if you stayed quietly in camp today, dear," said Mom, traitorously.

The betrayal was made much worse by the look of relief that crossed the boys' faces. "Oh, sure, Mom," she said savagely. "Lucky I brought my knitting, isn't it? Have fun fishing, boys. Just don't expect me to clean your catch, that's all."

The barb missed its mark. "Of course not. Everyone cleans his own." Denis sounded surprised.

"That's the rule, eh?"

"Of course."

What a family! She watched them walk eagerly across the glade and vanish into the bush. The men getting away from the tiresome women into their own cliquish little world. She had been wondering why on earth Mom had married Harry. Now she began to wonder why Harry had married Mom. Harry and the boys seemed like an indestructible threesome, needing no outsiders. As for looks, Mom was a fright this morning, with her negligee and mussed-up hair.

"What on earth was that about knitting?" Mom settled down at the table with a cup of coffee and lit a cigarette. "You never knit a thing in your life."

"Oh, Mom, give me a break! Can't you recognize sarcasm when you hear it?"

She could see Mom was prepared to be chatty, and she couldn't bear it. Furthermore there were two pans and the coffee pot to clean, besides the greasy plates and cutlery. *I'm darned if I'm going to volunteer,* she thought. *I never wanted to come in the first place.*

"I'm going for a walk." She got up quickly.

"Do you think that's wise? It would be so easy to get lost."

"Mom, if you think I'm going to sit around for a whole week while those three fish, you must be crazy! Don't worry. I'll stick to the road. I can hardly get lost then."

"I suppose not." Mom looked around at the alien forest with an expression on her face that made Lenora realize that she, too, was hating it.

"Mom, *why* did you agree to go along on this trip?"

"Agree? Why, I had to persuade Harry to *let* us come."

Lenora groaned. No wonder the boys hated having her along. She hadn't even been *invited.* "I suppose they've been camping together for the last hundred years or so, just the three of them?"

"Er…more or less." Mom had the grace to look guilty.

"And you had to shove us in? Mom, I thought it was Harry's idea."

"He thinks it is." Mom looked downright smug.

"But why were you so keen?"

"It seemed such a wonderful opportunity to bring us all together."

"Sure." Lenora looked dramatically around the empty campsite. "Anyway," she went on loftily, *"I* don't care what they do. I think all this family togetherness is overrated."

With the last word, she strolled off up the road with her hands in her jeans pockets, whistling. But of course Mom wouldn't *let* her have the last word. "Stay on the road," she yelled. "And look out for bears."

Lenora hesitated and then walked resolutely on. What a rotten thing to say to a person who was going exploring by herself. Look out for bears, indeed! *That was a joke, Mom, eh?* Sure it was just a joke. Mom wouldn't be lounging around in her night things with a cup of coffee and a cigarette if there really *were* any bears.

Walking along the road was boring, not really like exploring at all. Then she noticed a dirt track, narrower than the trunk road, off to the right. The track went in the opposite direction to the trail the boys had taken, so there was no chance they'd think she was following them. She'd *die* if they thought that.

She turned onto the track and began to walk briskly along, still whistling. Whenever she stopped whistling, just to moisten her lips, she noticed how very quiet it was. The trees almost met overhead. Incredibly tall, skinny lodgepole pines, far taller than the jack pines back east. An occasional spread of spruce.

You'd think that with all those trees there'd be birds shouting their heads off. Instead, it's as quiet as a graveyard. She shivered and pushed the thought out of her head. She went on walking and whistling. This road must go *somewhere.* She could see tire marks, and down in the low-lying places there were deep ruts. It would be a real wallow in wet weather, strictly for four-wheel-drives.

The trail was going uphill now and veering to the right. Maybe it was just a little circular tour that would bring her back to the campsite. She kind of hoped it would. The loneliness and silence got to her after a while. The trees crowded closely together. Once or twice she found herself stopping and looking over her shoulder, with the oddest feeling that someone was coming behind her. Someone or something. Some creature's eyes on her all the time. Something small that could flit from tree to tree like a ghost, something that she couldn't quite see.

When something actually *did* skitter across the trail in front of her, she screamed. She had to put her hands to her mouth to stop herself from going on screaming. Then she began to giggle. It was only a gopher. No, not a gopher. She'd been told that enough times by Mr. Know-it-all and his sons. It was a ground squirrel, a Richardson's ground squirrel.

It stopped a little way in front of her and stood on its hind legs with its tiny front paws tucked against its chest. She could see its bright eyes and the way its nose twitched nervously. Moving her hands slowly, she checked to feel if there was anything edible in her jeans pockets. But of course everything had been packed clean. Not so much as a left-over cookie crumb.

"Sorry," she told the ground squirrel. "Next time. Or come up to our camp and we'll give you a feast."

She spoke quite softly, but suddenly the ground squirrel flicked up its tail and scampered off. It wasn't her, she realized. Someone was coming towards her, down the trail. Someone. Or something. She turned, ready to run.

"Hey!"

Bears don't say "hey," she told herself, and turned around. It was a man, about twenty, very good-looking, with the beginnings of a black beard and with black curly hair. He was dressed in cut-offs and a T-shirt.

"Is anything wrong? I thought I heard a scream. And then voices. So I came along."

Lenora blushed. "Scream? No, I was just talking to a ground squirrel. Oh, dear." She blushed again. "That sounds dumb."

"Not a bit. I do it all the time. The only catch is they don't talk back. Talking to people is a great deal more interesting, but I don't have too many come this way. Would you like to come along and look at my place? It's just around the next bend."

All Mom's awful warnings came rushing into Lenora's head. "Oh, I don't know. I don't think so. I was just..." She turned and gestured down the path "...going back."

"I should tell you that my place is actually a forestry lookout tower. My name's Pete Diduck, by the way. I'm hired for the summer to watch out for lightning strikes in the forest reserve. If you're not scared of heights, there's a terrific view from the top of the tower."

"Of course I'm not scared. That'd be great. Oh, I'm Lenora Rydz."

"You're not camping alone, are you, Lenora?"

"My mom's back at camp. My stepfather and the boys are fishing."

"You really shouldn't go walking around in the bush alone, you know."

"I can look after myself."

"I'm sure you can. But suppose you hurt yourself, twisted your ankle, for instance. You'd have to wait for someone to come looking for you. If you travel in pairs there's always someone to go for help."

"I guess that makes sense. It was a bit dumb."

"You'll know for next time," he said comfortingly. "Here's the tower."

"Oh, wow!" She leaned back until her neck cracked and looked up and up.

"You'll get dizzy, doing that. Do you want to try the climb?"

"I...I guess so."

"You'll be fine. I'll have you go first on the way up and last on the way down. That way I can catch you if you *do* slip. But I'm sure you won't, and the view's worth the climb, I promise you."

For a second Lenora hesitated. Then she thought: *I'll have something exciting to tell the boys, something they haven't done. Something better than their dumb fishing.* "Okay, I'll risk it."

She climbed steadfastly, her eyes glued to the rung ahead, never once looking down. Though her heart was pounding and her palms were sweating, she made it up to the top without a slip.

"There, I knew you could do it. Now relax and take a look around. Isn't it great?"

Great wasn't the word for it. Lenora turned around and around, speechless. The forest rolled past the tower in a solid green mass to the mountains.

"That's Mount Dalhousie over there." Pete pointed. "And Obstruction Mountain down to the southwest. The really big peaks are out of sight, closer to the Banff–Jasper Highway."

"Oh, look, I can see the forestry trunk road. And that's the river we crossed."

"The Blackstone. If you turn around and look north you'll see the Brazeau. That's a big one. Great canoeing if you're good at white water. Over to the east there..." Lenora followed his pointed hand and saw a shimmer of blue. "That's the Brazeau Reservoir. Before they built the dam you could canoe right down to Edmonton with just a few portages. My dad used to do it all the time. Now it's a long hike around the dam site, but it's still worth doing."

"I used to canoe back in Ontario," Lenora said absently. She leaned her elbows on the guardrail and stared down. There was their campsite. She could see the station wagon, with the canoe still tied on the roof. And there was Mom. Tiny. Lost among the trees. What would it be like travelling on foot in this forest? She tried to imagine what it must have been like in the old days, before cars, but gave up. It was all too huge. You could go out of your mind all alone out there. She shivered suddenly.

"It is a bit breezy up here," Pete said. "Come on down and I'll walk you back to your camp."

"You don't have to do that, I'm fine."

"It's no bother. I should talk to your father anyway. There's an escaped prisoner. Or has the forest warden been up to your camp?"

"No. We just got in last night."

"I expect he'll be along later, but I'll warn your dad anyway."

The way back seemed very short. The trees were no longer scary, as she and Pete filled the silence with chatter. There was no one in sight when they got to the camp.

"I could make you some coffee," Lenora suggested politely, wondering if she could actually start the Coleman without blowing it up.

"That's all right. I should be getting back. I have a report to radio in. Every hour on the hour." He ran his hand along the hull of the canoe, which was still fastened to the top of the station wagon. "Nice. You're going to use it on the Brazeau?"

Lenora shrugged. "I don't know. Harry and the boys..."

"Tell them to be careful. It's been a wet summer. A lot of water going down."

"Okay. Thanks a lot. It was great seeing the view."

"You're welcome. Have a good holiday."

After Pete had left, Lenora decided that it was warm enough for sunbathing. She pulled her sleeping bag out of the tent and laid it on the grass. Mom was just getting dressed.

"So you're safely back. That's good. I thought I heard voices. Who was it?" Mom's voice was a bit sharp.

"Met the guy from the fire tower. He took me up to the top. Super view. I could see you." She skinned out of her jeans and into shorts and went out.

The sun baked down. After a while she pulled off her T-shirt and lay on her stomach in shorts and bra. This holiday wasn't turning out so badly after all. Pete was pretty neat. Maybe she could pay another visit to the tower tomorrow...

After half an hour she turned over on her back. She smoothed on more suntan oil and closed her eyes, feeling quite dopey with the sun. The grass hummed with late bees. It smelled hot and dry.

She was almost asleep when she heard Mom calling. "Lenora, put on your T-shirt, for goodness' sake."

"Mom, I'm perfectly respectable. If my bra had flowers on it or was purple or something, it'd be a bikini top. Actually I'm a darn sight more decent than if I *were* wearing a..."

"Put on your top!"

She heard voices and sat up to see Harry, Denis, and Brian appear out of the undergrowth at the top of the trail. She struggled into her T-shirt, blushing furiously. The cotton fabric stung as she dragged it over her shoulders. *Ouch! Too much sun*.

"Fish for lunch, anyone?" With a triumphant grin, Harry held up a string of trout.

Lenora cringed inside as Mom rushed over to admire them, cooing over the colours as if they were on display in an art gallery, for pete's sake, instead of being destined for the frying pan. She folded her sleeping bag and tossed it angrily into the tent.

Denis came over to her. "Look, I'm really sorry you couldn't come this morning. Dad's got his own way of doing things, you know. But I'm sure...it'll just take a little time."

"Don't worry about it. I couldn't care less. I had a fabulous morning."

"Oh. Good." Denis shuffled his feet. "Well, I'd better go stow my gear."

Wheels crunched on the dirt road and they turned. A green half-ton truck with mud tires pulled up in the clearing and a man in a green and tan uniform jumped out.

"You're not going to nail us for the trout, are you, officer?" Harry joked. "Licence in order." He patted his shirt pocket. "And under our day's limit." He held up the fish.

Glad of the chance to show off, thought Lenora spitefully.

"They're real beauties, sir. What did you use?" They went off into a technical discussion of which she didn't understand a single word. *Why does everything Harry do bug me so?*

"*I* know why you're here," she interrupted. "It's about the escaped prisoner, isn't it?"

He turned quickly, the fish forgotten. "Why, have you spotted someone? Missed clothing, food, any equipment?"

Lenora backed away, startled. "No. I didn't mean...it was Pete, from the lookout tower, who told me."

"What's all this about, officer?"

"Probably nothing to worry about, sir. Just an inmate

missing from the facility down the road. He didn't report back from a work party on Friday evening."

"You mean there's a convict at large in this forest?" Mom overreacted as usual, Lenora noticed. *"Here?* Oh, my God, Harry, let's go home."

"Take it easy, Hazel. What about it, officer? Is he a possible danger?"

"I shouldn't think so for a minute. I believe he's just a kid, seventeen or so."

"What did he do?" Mom's hands clasped together and Lenora knew she was thinking of all sorts of frightful things.

"He was driving the truck for a gang that broke into a Calgary warehouse."

"Well, we'll keep an eye out."

"Thank you, sir. If you should meet any other campers you might let them know. I'll be getting on."

"Have they got search parties looking for him?"

"They were stopping cars going east and west on the highway Friday night and Saturday morning. No hints of his whereabouts. That's why they think he's in the bush, and you can't search the bush, ma'am. It'd take thousands of men and you could still walk right by him. He'll have to surface some time, though. He'll need food. And the nights are getting snappy."

"But…"

"Really, ma'am, it's nothing to worry about. Just let us know if you see anything unusual."

He climbed into the cab of his truck. "Is he armed?" Mom yelled after him. *She's determined to make a drama of it, thought Lenora.*

"I don't know that I'd say *armed*, ma'am. But one of the work party's axes is missing."

In the silence after the truck squealed down the road Mom looked around dramatically. "Well, so this is the peaceful foothills country." She tried to laugh and lit another cigarette.

"Honestly, Hazel, the man's right. There's nothing to worry about. He'd have asked us to leave, if there were. Now, come on, let's get those trout in the frying pan before they spoil." Harry busied himself over the Coleman.

The fish were marvellous, Lenora had to admit, better than anything she'd tasted in Toronto restaurants, even if Harry and the boys had caught and cooked them.

"So when do I get to fish?"

Her question fell on dead air. Everyone lay around lazily.

"Well, I must do *something* this afternoon," she said into the silence.

"Can't you just relax and enjoy the peace and quiet, Nora?"

"There'll be plenty of time when I'm dead or too old to care, thanks very much, Harry. If fishing is what we came up here to do, then I want to learn to fish. So which of you gentlemen is going to teach me?"

She looked from Harry to Brian. Their faces were like doors slammed against her. *Oh, great.* "What about you, Denis?"

"I'd like…"

Brian interrupted. "We're pretty fussy about our gear, Nora. An amateur can jam the reel, tangle the line, lose a good fly…"

"Thanks a lot for the vote of confidence, Brian. I guess that goes for you, too, Harry? What did you have in mind for Mom and me to do while you were off fishing, huh?"

She could tell he hadn't really thought about it at all. It was just what she'd suspected when Mom had told her that *she* had persuaded Harry to bring them along. Camping was something he and the boys had done for years and years. Now that he'd married Mom, she and Mom were uncomfortably glued onto the Mathieson family without really being a part of it.

"Well, Mom," she challenged. "What are you going to do with your days? It's no good offering to take over the cooking or housekeeping. There's no housekeeping to do in two tents, and they all think your cooking's frightful."

There was a chrous of "That isn't true," "Hazel, we love your cooking," and "It's just that we want you to have a real holiday, too."

Mom interrupted. Her cheeks were very pink and her voice was a bit squeaky, the way it used to get with Daddy, but she didn't scream or anything. "That's quite enough, Lenora," she said quietly. "I really think this trip could be a valuable opportunity for us to get to know each other a little better, to really become a family."

"With us two twiddling our thumbs in camp and the guys off fishing or canoeing? You have to be joking! Honestly, Mom, I've had it. Will you please drive me back to the highway and I'll hitch a ride home. At least I can catch up on my swimming. A whole summer *wasted.*"

"It's not the whole summer, just a week, goofy!"

"I wouldn't let a daughter of mine hitch-hike, *or* stay in the house by herself," Harry put in.

Mom went bright red and began to splutter. Lenora found she was going to her rescue. "Well, you don't have a daughter, do you, Harry? Only sons. So you don't know how responsible a daughter can be, when she's given a chance."

Harry's face got red, too, and he lumbered to his feet in a menacing kind of way. *I suppose I've gone too far again*, thought Lenora. *But I don't care. I'm not going to let him boss me as if he were my dad. If he beats up on me, then Mom will be sorry she ever married him and we can go back to Ontario.* She stood glaring at Harry with her chin stuck out.

Before Harry could get his wits together, Denis had scrambled to his feet and was standing between the two of them. "Look, Dad, maybe I could take your old rod, the one you let me use, and maybe a few flies? I can take Nora upstream, where we were this morning, and teach her to cast."

For a moment it looked as if Harry were going to refuse. Then he shrugged. "If you want to risk it, I suppose I've no objection. But you're personally responsible for all my tackle, mind. And watch she doesn't put out your eyes."

"What was that crack supposed to mean?" Lenora demanded, as she and Denis walked up the trail towards the creek.

"What crack? Oh, you mean about my eyes? That was just Dad's joke."

"Funny kind of joke. As if I would!"

"It's just that when you're learning to cast, getting a hook in someone's eye *is* quite a likely accident."

"I'll be careful, honest."

"I'm sure you will. Look here, Nora, I know you and Dad are having problems. I just want to tell you that underneath he really is an okay guy. It hasn't been easy for him. My mother died when I was six and all his relatives told him he couldn't possibly handle a demanding job and bring up two kids as well. They said it'd be better for all of us if he put us up for adoption."

"That's awful! Didn't they offer to help?"

"Only with good advice. Anyway, Dad refused to listen to them. He gave up the army, bought a house in

Edmonton, and went into business for himself. And he taught himself how to cook — not just Kraft dinner and wieners and beans, but real gourmet stuff. He organized the house and the yard so that the three of us could look after everything. And yet he never missed showing up at school concerts and games and important stuff like that. The thing is, he did it when they all said he couldn't; so now he can't figure out why other people don't manage their lives as well as he does. It does make him a bit obnoxious at times, I admit."

"Okay, Denis. I'm glad you told me. I guess I can understand how he got to be the way he is, with the pressure of raising two kids and a new job and all. Only you're just about grown up, for crying out loud, yet he treats you as if he were the colonel and you were a new recruit. Doesn't that bug you?"

"I guess so. Sometimes. If I let it get to me." Denis stopped and put down his gear. "This is where we fished this morning. Actually, to tell you the truth, it's Brian who drives me up the wall."

"I can believe it. What a prig! And he doesn't have the excuse your dad does. Why do you stand for it?"

"It's not all black and white, the way you make out. He's got his good points, too. He's three years older than me, and Dad put a lot of responsibility on his shoulders when we were young — looking after me, for one."

"I think you should put a stop to it. It's not good for him. He's a terrible drip. I bet the girls really *despise* him."

"Brian's not that interested in a social life. He's into math and chess and..."

"Aha! Overcompensating. I told you..."

"You mustn't..." Denis tried to frown, but the

corners of his mouth twitched. "He really is bright. He's a member of Mensa."

"What's that?"

"You know — the organization for people with IQs in the top two per cent, over a hundred and thirty."

"What do they do? Get together and pat each other's egos?"

"It's not like that. I've been there. It's neat talking to people without having to get back to basics all the time."

"Denis." Lenora stared accusingly. "What's *your* IQ?"

"Oh, heck." He blushed.

"Come on."

"About a hundred and forty. Don't you *dare* let anyone in school know."

"Good grief, as if I would. No wonder I have so much trouble talking to you. I suppose Harry's way up in the stratosphere, too. Hey, did you catch that big word? Not bad for a moron like me."

"Lenora, will you quit? Now, pay attention. I'm going to teach you how to cast a dry fly. You will not blind me with the hook, nor will you catch the line in the trees or tangle it in the reel. In fact, you might even show Dad and Brian by catching a trout for dinner. Okay?"

"Okay, boss."

5

Sunday evening

As Denis walked along the creek with the fishing rod, Nora chattering beside him, he almost regretted his noble gesture. He'd only asked her because he didn't want a decent camping trip spoiled by her sulks and dramatic sighs, or by Dad in a rage. Anything for a quiet life. And, to be honest, it was a chance to show up Brian, whose preachy attitude was getting to be a bit much, even though he'd made excuses for it to Nora. *Heck, I'm almost fifteen now and he's only three years older. Where does he get off?*

But, amazingly, he had a great time. Nora only got the line tangled in the bushes once, and she made a game of it instead of acting upset.

"Help! Quick! Before your dad or Brian comes along and has us arrested." She acted real panicky and talked in a high, artificial voice. He started laughing so hard he couldn't help her untangle the line. Then she swatted his hands away. "I'll do it. I'll do it." Then they broke up again. It was insane.

He got her casting a nice clean length of line upstream and letting the current take the fly down. "Gently, gently," he said under his breath.

"I *am*," she whispered back. Then, "Why are we whispering?"

"I don't know. Dad and Brian always do. I guess loud noises scare off the fish."

She snorted and got the giggles again. Then she flicked the line upriver as neat as you please so the fly just touched the water. There was a swirl on the surface and the fly vanished.

"I've got a bite! I've got a bite!"

"Shh. Take it easy. Not yet, you haven't. Reel in carefully. Just till you can feel it. Know what I mean?"

"The line's alive. I *can* feel it. Oh, I know it's a big one! Huge." The line ran suddenly out and, without his having to tell her, she began to reel in again. The rod tip bent. It *was* a big one.

"Easy. Let the line out a bit." Denis wanted her to make a good catch, but part of him was even more anxious about Dad's line and fly. "Ease off," he pleaded, but she just shook her head.

She moved forward until she was standing in the shallows, icy water frothing around her shins. She tossed her long fair hair back and bit the tip of her tongue, a frown of concentration on her forehead. Then she played the fish like a pro. It must have been ten minutes before it was all over and she was able to bring the exhausted trout into the shallow water where Denis could skim the net under it and lift it, wriggling and jumping, from the water. A kilo and a half, at least, he thought, with a pang of envy. Better than his catch that morning.

"I did it! I did it!" She was grinning from ear to ear. "I knew I could. Oh, Denis, don't take it out of the water. Can you get the hook out without hurting it?"

"I guess so."

"Then let it go."

"But it's a huge one...and they'll *never* believe us if they don't see it for themselves."

"I don't care. I did it. That's all that matters. Please, Denis."

So he gently eased the hook out of the jaw and let the great trout go. He could feel its length along his hand. Then there was a swirl and it was gone.

Lenora collapsed on the grass and began to rub her legs. "That was fantastic. What a rush! Gee, my legs are absolutely freezing."

"Let me." He knelt beside her and began to rub some warmth back into her feet. They were small and white with neat straight toes. They could practically fit in his hand. His head suddenly felt swimmy and he stood up. "We'd better go back. You don't want to catch cold."

"You're the one who sounds like you're catching cold. What's the matter? Your voice has gone all funny."

"Nothing." He turned and walked away from her, a dozen paces upstream. When he looked back she was sitting with her back against a tree. Her fair hair caught a sunbeam and she looked as if she were made out of golden light.

She squinted up at him against the brightness. "Stop hovering and park yourself, Denis. I want to talk to you."

He squatted with his back to the sun. He could see her, but she couldn't really see him. "Okay. Shoot."

"I want to suggest an alliance. You and me against Brian."

"I thought this vacation was supposed to promote togetherness."

"That's just my mom's muddled thinking. Actually, it'll probably promote war, which should be obvious to a bright boy like you. And I need an ally."

"Against my own brother? That's not very nice."

"It's for your own good. And his. Denis, you're fifteen years old."

"Well, almost. Next month."

"So it's time you became independent. I've noticed how you run around after Brian, do what he says, imitate the way he says things, even copy his school project."

Denis's cheeks grew hot. He was suddenly furious at Lenora for criticizing him, and furious with himself for caring a hoot what she thought. He found himself blustering. "At Rocky Mountain House? Well, why not? It was a darn good idea."

"Sure. But not *that* good. I bet if you gave yourself half a chance you could think up something every bit as original. But how are you going to, if you get in the habit of being Brian's carbon copy?"

He didn't know what to make of her. She had a hell of a nerve, barging into his family and telling him how to behave. He should really tell her off. But...

As he hesitated, she grinned. She had a very nice smile. It lit up her whole face, which looked kind of heavy and dull when she was in a sulky mood. "So what about it, Denis? Are we allies?"

"I'll think about it, Nora."

"And you can start by not calling me Nora. I hate it with a passion. Nobody *ever* called me Nora till your father started doing it."

"Okay, okay. I'll think about what you said, *Lenora*. Now, do you want to fish some more?"

"No, thanks. I'll never match that experience, not in a million years."

"Then maybe we should go back." He felt prickly and irritated, half wanting to show off and do something dumb that would make her admire him, half wishing the old days were back when life was peaceful and he knew where he stood. Dad and Brian. Just the three of them.

The camp was in a state of organized turmoil. "What's going on, Dad?"

"Oh, glad you're back, son. Go help Brian strike the tents. We're going up to the Brazeau campground today instead of Wednesday." Dad answered his question with an order. *As if he were the colonel and you a new recruit.* Yes, it did bug him, he realized.

"But I thought we'd planned to have at least three days' fishing along Brown Creek before..."

"There's been a change of plan. Don't argue, boy. Just do as you're told."

"Thanks for asking my opinion," he muttered as he went to help Brian.

"And don't mutter!"

"So what's up?" he asked Brian, as they worked together collapsing and folding the tents.

"You heard Dad, little brother."

"Quit calling me that."

"Okay, okay. No need to get tense. If you must know, Dad and Hazel had a private talk and told me we were moving. I think they decided that sitting around was a bit much for us — all together — if you get me. So we're cutting short the fishing here and heading up to the Brazeau River for the canoeing part of the trip."

"Oh, great! I'm really looking forward to that." Denis felt a bit mollified. "But I think he should have asked us first. It'd have been a bit more democratic, wouldn't it?"

"You know Dad. Actually, I think Hazel isn't too keen on Nora getting to know that guy at the lookout tower — nervous about her little girl." He laughed in a disparaging way that made Denis want to hit him. "Come on, stop staring and help me load these into the station wagon."

They were on the road within an hour. Dad's usual efficiency, thought Denis with grudging admiration.

"So how was the fishing, Nora?" Brian's voice was at its most sarcastic. "Did you catch a minnow or just a tree?"

"I caught a huge brown trout. It must have weighed a kilo and a half at least."

"Yeah?"

"Tell him, Denis."

He described exactly how she had caught the fish, his face getting hot as Brian's eyebrow slowly went up.

"So where is this great trophy, Nora?"

"I let it go. I didn't want to kill it or eat it. I just wanted to prove that I could fish. And I *can*."

"Did you cook that story up between you?" Brian spoke quietly, but not very quietly, in Denis's ear.

"Of course not. What a fink you are, Brian."

They drove in silence the rest of the way up the forestry trunk road to the Brazeau River campground. It wasn't much more than a half-hour drive, but they had the business of unpacking and getting the tents up again.

There was a well-built stone fireplace in the middle of the clearing, so they built a fire and baked potatoes in the embers and fried steaks out of the big cooler.

"I'm glad the fire risk is low and we *can* have a fire." Hazel snuggled up to Harry. "There's nothing as romantic as a fire, is there, sweetie?"

"Makes better coffee than the Coleman, that's for sure," was all that Harry said, and Denis saw him move away from Hazel to refill his mug.

Denis saw Lenora flush, jump up, and walk away. He wanted to go after her, tell her not to be embarrassed about Hazel, tell her there were plenty of times when the old man embarrassed the heck out of him. He wanted to reassure her that their new family would be okay, once they gave it a chance, that this camping trip didn't count. But Brian's eyes were on him and he found himself pretending that he was just reaching for another cup of coffee.

"Oh, you finally unloaded the canoe. I was wondering if it was going to spend the whole week on the top of the station wagon." Lenora ran her hand over the hull. "Aluminum?" She sounded disapproving.

"A darn sight more serviceable than chestnut, and stronger than fibreglass. But what do you know about canoes, Nora?" Brian looked down his long nose, suddenly so like Dad that Denis let out an involuntary snort of laughter. Then he felt a kind of chill. *Yes, she was right. Brian was getting more like Dad every day. That was a pretty terrifying thought.*

"So what do you know about canoes?" Brian repeated.

"Enough. I've done a lot of canoeing up in the Gatineau lakes. And on the Ottawa River. Shot the Chaudière Rapids a couple of times. That was a blast."

"Bow or stern?"

"Huh?"

"Were you paddling bow or stern when you shot the rapids?"

"Neither, actually. I was number three on that trip. In the middle."

Brian smiled. It was that smile that made Denis decide once and for all that he was going to be Lenora's ally. He saw her hands double into fists as she reacted to Brian's expression and tone.

"I guess we're talking real macho stuff," she said stiffly. "Are Alberta rivers that different from Ontario ones? White water's still white water, and I suppose a canoe still behaves like a canoe."

Before Brian could demolish her, Denis rushed in to explain. "It's just that in the foothills the rivers tend to be very fast — all that energy coming down from the Rockies — and they can change level and speed pretty rapidly after a rainstorm. It's a huge catchment area, all funnelling into three or four rivers."

"Sounds like fun! When are we going to have a crack at it? Tomorrow?"

"No, Nora." Harry interrupted. "Early Tuesday Brian and I plan to take the canoe down the Brazeau to the dam and portage over into the North Saskatchewan. We'll take it easy, do some fishing on the way down. You can pick us up in Emily Murphy Park on Saturday."

"'Brian and I'?" Denis got slowly to his feet. His legs were shaking and it was hard to keep his voice steady. "What do you mean, 'Brian and I'? What about *me*?"

"You'll stay on till Friday, look after the girls. Then you can drive up to Edson, camp along the Jasper trail if you want, and pick us up around noon on Saturday."

"But, Dad, we've been planning a river trip for the three of us for years and years. And suddenly I'm not even part of it…and you didn't even talk to me about it…it's not *fair*."

"Not fair? That doesn't sound like a fifteen-year-old man, son. Someone should stay with Hazel and Nora, make sure they're all right."

"But why me, why not Brian?"

"Because you're not nearly as strong a paddler as I am, little brother."

"It isn't fair. Brian, you've had first crack at everything ever since I…"

"That's enough, son. You're to stay and that's it. Next year, perhaps."

"*Perhaps*! Thanks, Dad. Thanks a whole lot."

Denis walked out of the camp and up the road to the bridge. He was shaking with anger, helpless anger. He snatched up a branch and slashed at the bushes, taking it out on the weeds. At the bridge he leaned over the parapet and looked down at the dark water. *Hard to see how fast it's moving in the twilight.* He threw down his branch. It swirled, caught the main current, and hurtled downstream.

Feet crunched behind him. He turned, ready for battle, but it was Lenora.

She stopped. "I won't stay if you'd rather be alone."

"No, it's okay."

"I'm sorry you're stuck with looking after us."

"It's not that. I'd be glad to. It's just…all the talk we'd had about the canoe trip. He never once said it didn't mean me, too. I took it for granted. We've never had an overnight river trip before. You've got to organize someone to drive the car back, you see, and pick you up at the other end."

"Didn't your Dad have friends he could ask along?"

"He's always been a bit of a loner, especially since leaving the army. He doesn't quite trust other people."

Lenora began to laugh. "I'm sorry. But how devious. Once Mom and I became part of the family, he must have realized he had a driver at last. How *convenient*."

Denis could feel himself blushing. He muttered something about Hazel so stupid he stopped in mid-sentence.

"Wait a minute. That doesn't make sense. Mom said she had to persuade Harry to take us…"

"Yeah, well…"

"I get it. Her being able to drive the station wagon back was the inducement. Right?"

Denis nodded, unable to think of a thing to say.

"And of course the arrangement didn't bother you, leaving Mom and me on our own in this dumb forest for four days? Just as long as you could tag along with Daddy and brother Brian."

He winced at her tone. "We weren't supposed to go

till Wednesday," he said weakly. "But I guess you're right. It wasn't fair. But it seemed like one last chance to go back to the old days, when there were just the three of us."

"Only your dad changed his mind and now he doesn't want Mom and me to be alone. So *you're* stuck with playing nursemaid. No way Brian would ever offer. The only person Brian's going to look out for is Brian. You should know that by now. It's about time you smartened up and showed them that you're somebody, too."

"How?"

"By making some dramatic statement."

"I've told them..."

"Words! You're going to have to *do* something."

"Like what?"

"Oh, I don't know. Something like...like sneaking a canoe trip before they've had a chance to take off. Oh, Denis!" She grabbed his arm. Her eyes were shining in the twilight. "What a fantastic idea. Let's!"

"You mean...take off downriver? That's crazy! How would we ever get the canoe back up to the camp?"

"Couldn't we paddle upstream?"

"Against that current? Come on!"

"Well, I suppose if it got too tough we could portage back to the road. But all the early explorers and surveyors went upriver, didn't they? And they had all that heavy surveying equipment to haul along, and food for months and months."

"And they also had strong native paddlers and lots of muscle power over the portages..."

"...while we've got the two of us and an empty canoe. Oh, come on, Denis. Just a couple of kilometres downriver and back. I'm longing to see what's around that corner. I think I'll die of boredom if something interesting doesn't happen soon."

"It's a crazy idea, Lenora. There's no way. Anyway, we'll never get a chance of getting hold of the canoe without the others seeing us. So there you are."

Dad put a hand on Denis's shoulder as they got ready for bed. "I hope you're not too disappointed, son."

He shrugged the hand off angrily. "Of course I am, Dad. What'd you think? I'd been looking forward to the trip ever since we first planned it. And I'm mad you didn't even *ask* me first."

"Hazel and I had a bit of an argument when you and Nora were fishing, you know how these things are. Taking off early seemed the best way out of a difficult situation."

"But why leave me behind?"

"Hazel was concerned about being alone with Nora; she's worried about that escaped prisoner."

"What? Oh, yes, I'd forgotten. Good grief, Dad..."

"I know. I told her that he'd be a hundred, two hundred kilometres away from here. But...well, that's what the argument was about, actually. I need someone responsible to look after Hazel and Nora. Calm their fears and so on. I know I can trust you, my boy."

"Couldn't you trust Brian? Is that what you're saying?"

"Don't be ridiculous. You know perfectly well what I mean."

"Then couldn't Brian and I at least have tossed a coin? It isn't fair."

"It's just a few days."

"That's not the point, Dad. You *promised* us this trip. You said: Don't make a fuss if the girls come too. Having Hazel along means we can make the whole trip downriver at last. Now suddenly I'm expendable. I suppose Brian told you I'd better stay?"

"Well…"

"Thanks, Dad." He didn't even try to keep the bitterness out of his voice.

"Next trip, son. I promise."

Denis deliberately yawned and turned his back. "Sure, Dad."

But though he lay still in his sleeping bag, he couldn't sleep. Brian came into the tent and settled down. Denis could hear their even breathing as they slept. He turned over and back again. He angrily remembered every single time Brian had scored over him, every time Brian had been chosen.

Lenora's right, he thought. *I'm going to have to do something dramatic, just to prove that those two can't go on walking all over me for ever.*

He sat up, wriggled out of his sleeping bag, and crept out of the tent. It was very quiet. The stars blazed down steadily, no heat shimmer, no city lights to interfere. As he looked up, idly identifying stars and constellations, a shooting star flared briefly and then died. Then another. Coming roughly out of the northeast. That would be the Perseids, wouldn't it? Tonight was the 12th of August, or was it the 13th? It was easy to lose track of time without newspapers or radios to cut up and name the days. He watched the sky peacefully for about half an hour, leaning against the side panel of the station wagon.

The moon crept over the trees to the east and swamped the stars. The blackness of the forest took on a shape, the sombre bulk of spruce and pine solid in the cold white moonlight. Impulsively he walked up the road to the river, his bare feet curling back from the cold stones.

The river was a silver ribbon, unwinding beneath the bridge and vanishing to the left downstream. It didn't look too fast, and it would be fun to see what was around that bend over there. There'd be no harm in taking a look at the topographical map, and maybe a glance at the handbook of Alberta rivers. The book and map were in the back of the station wagon. Next to the cooler.

He padded on cold bare feet back to the campsite. There was a flashlight just inside the tent door. He held his breath as his fingers groped for it. Dad's breathing was even. So was Brian's. Neither stirred.

Opening the tailgate of the station wagon made an appalling amount of noise. He froze, trying to think of a plausible excuse for what he was doing. There was a sleepy mutter from one of the tents. Then silence.

The moon hung over his shoulder. It was so bright that he practically didn't need a flashlight. Denis looked at the map. The river bent to right and left and back again, half a dozen bends in less than a kilometre.

There were no rapids marked on the map, but the river banks were steep. If they got into trouble...but why should they? If they paddled down to this last loop, they'd have a very good workout and still have only a kilometre to portage back. And how satisfying it would be to thumb his nose at Dad and the increasingly insufferable Brian. And Lenora would approve. For some reason this was suddenly important.

He folded the map, seeing in his mind's eye the bends of the river. Lucky he had a good memory, almost photographic. Now for a quick look at Dad's handbook. He bent over the tailgate of the station wagon, poking around and flashing his light into the corners.

There it was, stuck in the corner between the cooler and the curve of the wheel well. He tucked the flashlight under his arm and began to turn the pages. *Brazeau, Brazeau. Here we are. Headwaters...no. Second reach...oh, come on, where's the place?*

"Denis?"

He threw the book back into the car and as quietly as he could eased the tailgate closed. On the balls of his feet he sprinted across the campground and was strolling back to the tent when Brian poked his head out.

"What on earth are you doing?"

"Just been to the can. Shut up, you'll wake everyone up shouting like that."

"Saw you'd gone and started worrying about bears."

"Dear elder brother, I am practically fifteen years old and I'm capable of finding the outhouse by myself and getting back. If you'll move out of the doorway I can get in. I'm freezing."

He remembered to turn off the flashlight. Brian took it out of his hands and flashed it back on just as Denis was crawling into his sleeping bag. "You'd think you'd been for a hike. Your feet are filthy. You'll get your bag in a mess."

The last word, as usual, thought Denis, but less resentfully than before. In his mind's eye flashed the words he had gleaned from the book on the Brazeau River just as Brian had called out. "Below this point the river is choppy, with frequent easy rapids characterized by large waves but few rocks."

If they leave Lenora and me alone for long enough so we can grab the canoe and take off, I'll do it. He imagined them negotiating the bends and the "frequent easy rapids" and coming back to camp in triumph. *It'll surprise the heck out of Dad and Brian and show Lenora I can stand up for myself,* he thought sleepily. *And if we can't get the canoe she won't be able to say I shirked it. So I win either way. I'll tell her first thing in the morning.* Feeling mightily pleased with himself, Denis fell asleep.

6

Sunday

Isaac woke at sunrise. He was shivering with cold and his stomach hurt, though he told himself that it was no worse than it had been the night before. He lay, still sleepy, dazedly staring up into the spruce tree under which he had slept. Like a tipi, a huge tipi in an encampment of thousands of tipis. Like the old days his grandmother used to talk about, not her time, but the stories *her* grandmother had told her.

He crawled from under the spiky boughs, feeling the nearness of his people all around him, a warm, secure feeling. He stood straight and looked around. There was nothing there, just a little morning mist smoking among the silent trees. What was he doing here? He shook his head to clear it and remembered where he was going, what he was doing. He smoothed his socks carefully so there were no wrinkles in them and pushed his feet into his work boots. Then he picked up his friend the axe, felt for the stone in his pocket, and began to walk north.

The hills closed in about him as he walked. Before long he crossed a creek. He ran his tongue over his dry, cracked lips and knelt beside the water. He washed his face, but he would drink nothing, though his body was screaming for water. Part of him knew that what he was doing was crazy, that to go on walking at yesterday's pace without water was to build up all sorts of poisons in his mucles. The other part of him knew only the vow he had made in the medicine lodge. To abstain from food and water until he found his spirit.

In the old days, Grandmother had said, a youth would go to seek his spirit, purifying his mind and body by fasting. When his spirit showed itself, whether it was rabbit or bear, eagle or deer, the young man would know that he was to live under the protection of that animal, learning its cunning or strength, its keen eyes or its swiftness.

But that was in the past. Could the spirit come to him in the *now* world? Or was he crazy?

In the *now* world, he walked doggedly along the trail until he came, after a couple of kilometres, to the next fork. It was clear that this was the fork the old man had spoken of. The path split into a T, to left and right. Directly ahead of him loomed a thousand metres of hill. To his right a small river flowed east and the path sidled along the gap it had eroded in the hills.

He remembered that he must turn west, towards the mountains again, just for a short time, to avoid a campground. That was all right. The sun was just above the trees and the sky was a pale, washed-out blue. In spite of his cold, stiff muscles he trudged steadily on, over the edge of a hill, following to its source some nameless little creek.

Creeks like this had fed the river and lake where Grandmother lived. Trout from the streams, roots and berries from the bush. Nothing to buy but flour, tea, and sugar. What a life!

Yeah, said his other half. *But what is your stomach dreaming about now? Not berries for sure. A thick, juicy hamburger with masses of onions and mounds of french fries.*

When Mom had come to take him he'd yelled and kicked.

"Won't go. Won't leave Grandmother."

"I'm your mom and you're coming with me, so shut up."

"Let the boy stay, Marie. He's happy here."

"Happy? Till when? You still don't understand, Ma. You can't stay here any more. They'll throw you out and then what'll happen to the boy?" And with that his mom had tossed him into the car and they had bumped along the track to the trail to town, with him crying and carrying on.

She'd stopped at a Burger King and Isaac had had his first hamburger. The tears had dried up and he'd smiled at Mom. She'd smiled back, her eyes twinkling under her dark curls — how had her hair got fuzzy like that? he'd wondered — and her gold earrings dancing. She'd worn a pink frilly blouse and blue jeans and she was different from anyone Isaac had ever seen. By the time they'd reached the rooming house in Edmonton he was pretty excited about his new life.

What a fool I was, thought Isaac. He stood for a while, catching his breath, looking across the limitless spread of pine and spruce. Then he walked doggedly on, angry with the six-year-old self who'd been bribed with a hamburger.

The trail led more or less downhill, and the little creek that was its companion became a river as more and more creeks tumbled down from the high country to his right to join it. As the growing river filled the narrow valley or spread out into low and swampy places, his path wandered to and fro across it. He was travelling more or less east now and the sun was edging towards the mountains behind him. He reckoned he'd travelled fifty, sixty kilometres in the past two days, following the trail. How close he was, as the crow flies, to the river, he had no idea.

Another day was almost over, though the true sunset wouldn't happen for another couple of hours and it would be light enough to walk for some time after that. Another day...what was today? Sunday?

He had broken away from the work party on Friday night. That other life was like a dream now. The realities were the trees around him, the sky above his head, the trail stretching on before him. *Tomorrow I cross the forestry trunk road*, he told himself. *Tomorrow I must reach the Brazeau River. I will be close to the place of my grandmother. Then I will know what to do*.

The trail crossed and recrossed the river on footbridges made of neatly laid logs. He had helped repair bridges like that, somewhere, a long time ago. He felt the weight in his right hand and remembered. Yes, he had fixed them with this axe. The weight felt good. The axe was a companion, like the lucky stone the old man had given him. His left hand went up to his shirt pocket to touch the lump. Yes, it was safe, his luck.

He came upon the dry-weather road and turned north. The surface was good and he strode along, his thoughts for company. Ten years he'd stayed with Mom, ten years of trailing from one rooming house to another. Ten years of school...

"Isaac, get back in your seat."

"But there's a bird out there. Didn't you see it?"

"Isaac, *will* you stop looking out of the window and pay attention."

His bottom grew sore from sitting on a hard chair and his head ached from staring at the blackboard. He hated the sour smells of sweat and stale clothing and chalk dust, and he longed for Grandmother. *But I'll never get back. I'll never see her again*. He stopped looking out the window and ducked his head down so the other kids wouldn't see he was crying.

Isaac strode on, the cloak of darkness sinking lower and lower about him, trying to walk away from the memory of the pain and the powerlessness of being a child, until he suddenly sprawled over an exposed tree root.

Enough, his body told him. *If you twist an ankle what use will you be? How will you find your grandmother's place with a broken leg, huh?*

But the white man's road made him nervous. He knew he would not be able to sleep close to it, so when it intersected a seismograph line cutting southwest to northeast through the forest, he stepped thankfully off the hard clay onto the grass. This was man-made, too, but it felt friendly. He forced his body to walk along it till he was out of sight of the road. Only then did he step away from the cut into the forest, looking for a comforting cedar or a spruce for his night's shelter.

He longed desperately to light a fire, not just for its warmth but for its comfort. But suppose they were out with helicopters looking for him? Or what if an observer from a fire tower saw the light? The tiniest spark would show up in the darkness of the night forest.

He scratched a blaze along the ground, pointing back towards the trail he had just left. It would be stupid to get turned around in the morning and go wandering off. Then he crept under the sheltering boughs of a great cedar. They were like arms reaching out to welcome him. How tired he was. How cold.

Idly he swept fallen brown needles into a pile, imagining they were his fire. He held out his hands to warm them over the invisible blaze. He could almost smell the pungent smell of woodsmoke. The light — he could almost see the light — made a sacred circle in the centre of which he sat, protected.

"Oh, spirit, where are you?" he cried out loud. His voice was swallowed up by the trees, leaving not even an echo. "There is only one more day left. I have seen nothing. I have heard nothing. I am tired and cold. I am hungry and so thirsty. Oh, spirit, help me."

Did something move among the dark shadows? For an instant he saw the face of the old native down on the Kootenay plains. Then it turned into the face of the old man in the medicine lodge...no, three old men. But they weren't old, they were his age, just boys. The faces of Ben, Moses, Jim.

"Come on, man. You can't hang around the bus depot all day."

"I haven't got a place to stay. No bread." His lips moved as he remembered what he had said. "If I could just get back to Edmonton..."

They'd looked at each other. Just a flash. If he had been smarter, he'd have known that they were up to no good. But he was a dumb country kid, off the reserve. He'd worked at the car wash. Now that job was gone and there seemed to be no others.

"Hey, come on. We'll buy you a drink. You can shack up with us. Just a couple of blankets on the floor, okay?"

"Sure. Thanks."

"Maybe we can put some work your way," Ben had said.

"Yeah, you bet." Moses had glanced at Jim and Ben and the three of them had nodded, grinning like jack-o'-lanterns. How could he have believed that guys like them could ever be his *friends*?

They'd treated him to beer and french fries. Jeez, it was good to feel his stomach stretched again. But instead of taking him home they'd started talking about a party.

"I don't want to go to a party. I mean, look at me, guys. I'm a mess."

"That's okay. It's nothing fancy. Come on, what's the matter with you? Ain't our company good enough?"

"Yeah, man," the other two had chorused. "What's the matter with you?" He could see their heads now, bobbing up and down like pale balloons among the dark trees.

They'd pushed him into the cab of a pick-up.

"Whose truck is this?" he'd asked, knowing there was something fishy, wanting out, but not wanting to be ungrateful. They *had* bought his beer and paid for his french fries. They were the only people who'd acted friendly in weeks.

"A guy we know. We'll meet him at the party."

"Yeah." The others had nodded and then Moses and Ben had climbed up beside him and they'd started driving around Calgary until he was completely lost.

"But what about Jim? Isn't he coming?"

"Sure. He's coming later."

Then Moses had pulled over in a laneway. "Hold on for a minute. Keep a lookout. We got to pick up something for the party." He and Ben had piled out and vanished into the darkness, leaving him in the truck with the engine running noisily.

"Look out for what?" he'd called after them. Had that been a laugh from down the dark laneway?

Why hadn't he left the truck and walked away? Was he that dumb? Or was he so lonely for friends that he didn't *want* to know what they were up to?

He could feel his heart thudding now as it had thudded back then while he sat in the truck waiting, waiting for the guys to come back. Waiting to be caught in the bright lights like a rabbit, to be hauled out, searched, questioned.

"Whose truck is that? Is it yours? Were you driving? Why were you parked there?"

And slowly, out of the pelter of questions, the finger-printing and photographing, one clear picture emerging. A warehouse full of radios and stereo equipment, broken into. A stolen truck outside, with him sitting in it.

Moses, Ben, and Jim had got clean away with a whole load of stuff in the truck Jim must have been driving. Isaac had been nothing but a decoy to occupy the police.

Stupid. Stupid...

The pale, grinning faces under the dark cedar boughs nodded in agreement.

"Go away," he screamed. "Get out of my head." He swept away the pile of needles, his cold dark fire, and buried his face in the dirt.

7

Monday morning

A full-fledged row exploded right after breakfast on Monday.

"Why on earth couldn't you have told me *yesterday* that you were going to run out of cigarettes? Now we're even further from a store," Harry fumed.

"I thought there was a carton in the car. I could have sworn…" Mom ran a hand through her hair.

"Sweetheart, you *did* promise you'd cut back. Your lungs, your heart, your blood pressure…"

"Statistically…" Brian interrupted.

"Shut up," his father said, not even looking at him. "Now, Hazel…"

"It's *my* heart, *my* blood pressure, *my* lungs. And it's also my mind. Why did I ever listen to you? It was going to be so relaxing out in the bush. All this fresh air, this peace, this calm. I wouldn't even *want* to smoke."

"But it *is* relaxing…don't tell me you can't feel the difference. Come on, Hazel."

"Sure. With escaped prisoners running around with axes. With my daughter wandering off into the bush, striking up friendships with strange young men. With all of us at each other's throats. It's like a zoo. I've got to have a smoke if I'm going to keep my sanity."

"Dad, it's only fifty-four kilometres up the road to

Robb. There's a store there," Denis put in cautiously.

"It's still a ludicrous distance to go for..."

"...I'm not asking you to waste your precious day, Harry. Go and fish, go on. Enjoy yourself. And you can make your own lunch, too. It's obvious that you don't need me for anything except to drive the station wagon home..."

Lenora hid a smile behind a casual hand. So that had got to Mom in the end, too, had it? The only thing she couldn't understand was that Mom had expected this holiday to be wonderful. *She* had known it wouldn't work, so why hadn't Mom?

"So give me the keys, Harry. I'll go myself."

"I thought you were scared of the convict?"

"Not while I'm driving, I'm not. It's staying in camp, just me and Lenora, that I object to. Give me the keys, Harry." She held out her hand.

Lenora could see Harry's face getting redder. She could imagine what was going on in his mind: to go fishing and have Mom throw his indifference in his face any time she wanted an argument, or to give up fishing for the morning and...

"Oh, heck, I might as well take you myself. Is there anything else we're running out of? Just to make the trip worthwhile." He forced a smile. "More pop, kids? Want to come along for the ride?"

Lenora held her breath and willed Denis to say the right thing.

"Lenora and I thought we might try fishing again, Dad, if it's all right with you."

Thank goodness. Lenora let her breath out thankfully. *I was scared he wouldn't catch on.*

"Mind you don't teach her a lot of bad habits. Maybe I should come along to keep an eye on you," Brian suggested officiously.

Lenora felt her face sag. Oh, double darn! She caught Mom's eye in a desperate plea. *Do something!*

At least being married to Harry hadn't changed Mom completely. She could still recognize an SOS. Lenora couldn't help admiring the way she turned to Brian and put her hand on his arm. "Why don't you come along with us, Brian? If the store in Robb is big enough, I might be able to pick up some fishing tackle of my own. You can advise me."

"What about *my* advice, eh, Hazel?"

"Oh, you, Harry! Your idea of what will do starts at a couple of hundred dollars. What about it, Brian?"

Brian's smug face mirrored his struggle between showing off to his new stepmother or staying behind to boss his kid brother. The stepmother won. "I'd be glad to help, Hazel."

Thanks, Mom, thanks, Lenora said to herself. Out loud she encouraged them on their way. "Leave the breakfast things. We'll do them."

"All right. Take care. Are you sure you'll be all right?" Mom turned, her hand on the station-wagon door.

"Mom, we're just going fishing. Don't *fuss*."

They watched Harry edge the station wagon off the grass and onto the road. He slowly drove away from the campsite. Lenora could hear the pebbles crunch under the car wheels and the engine labour on the slope beyond the bridge. Then blessed silence flooded in. Silence and the scream of a jay challenging them for the breakfast leftovers. She threw it a crust.

"Wow, what a fantastic piece of luck!" Denis said.

"What do you mean — luck?"

"You mean you..."

Lenora ducked into her tent and came out brandishing a cigarette carton, unopened. "I nicked it first thing this morning, while Mom was washing, and hid it under my sleeping bag. I was terrified that she'd really start hunting for it."

Denis stared at her. She was standing in the sun, dressed in a white top and yellow shorts, her pale hair floating around her shoulders.

"What's the matter? You think I shouldn't have done it, don't you? Well, I'm sorry, but I don't care. Sometimes you can't just *dream* about the things you want. You've got to *make* them happen." She stuck her chin up and Denis wondered why he'd ever thought of her as a wishy-washy kid.

"So, are we going canoeing or aren't we?"

"Well…" She was as bad as Brian. It was always the same. The stronger other people were, the weaker and more irresolute he felt. "I don't know…"

"You *promised*. If we got the chance to be on our own, you said."

"I meant if it just happened. I'm not sure it counts if you go and make it happen."

"Oh, don't split hairs, Denis. You should be glad. We've got all that time. Look, we know they can't get back for three hours minimum, if the road's anything like the way it was up here. And that doesn't include the time they'll spend looking at fishing gear."

"Well, okay," he said reluctantly. *I'm going to regret it,* he thought, with that familiar feeling of being backed into a corner. "You're *sure* you know how to handle a canoe?"

"You bet. I've had lessons and lots of practice."

"All right, then. I just had time for a glance at the map and guidebook before Brian came snooping, but it seems there's a ten-kilometre stretch downstream from the bridge that's okay. Some choppiness and easy rapids in the last four. At that point the river heads east and we'll have to beach the canoe and portage back."

"Ouch! A ten-kilometre portage? You're joking!"

"Want to change your mind?"

"No way! But we don't have to go *that* far, do we?"

"Actually, by canoeing ten kilometres, we finish up close to home. The river hairpins like mad and after ten kilometres it's only about fifteen hundred metres below our camp. Can you handle that?"

"Sure I can. We had portages much longer than that between some of the Gatineau lakes. I'll even carry the canoe halfway, if you like."

"We'll see. All right, let's get going."

"Stop jumping around like a jack-rabbit. I promised we'd clean up the breakfast dishes, remember?"

"Good grief!" He felt that his courage wouldn't return until he was actually on the water. Right now there was still time to change his mind, to decide whether he was going to be an idiot or not. Once on the water, it would be too late for decisions like that. They'd be committed.

"They can't possibly be back for at least three hours. Come on. There's hot water in the kettle. And you've told me enough times that the campsite must be clean, so as not to encourage bears. We'll clean up and store everything safely away. It won't take long."

After the dishes were done, the stove put away, and the cloth hung on a bush to dry, Lenora found herself fussing around the camp, straightening sleeping bags, fastening the tent flaps. Her eye caught a chocolate bar and she grabbed it and shoved it into one shirt pocket, buttoning the flap down carefully.

"Aren't you ready yet?"

"You bet. Let's go!"

"Life jackets..." he remembered. "Oh, I hope they're not still in the station wagon. We can't go if..."

"Don't worry. They're in our tent. Here."

"If you carry them and the fishing rods and flies I'll take the canoe. Give me a hand."

She tucked the flies with some caution into her other pocket, and propped the bow of the canoe up so that Denis could walk under it and take the weight of it on his shoulders, the lashed paddles acting as a yoke. She did it competently and without fuss. *It's going to be okay*, Denis thought. *She knows what she's doing.*

They tramped up the road to the bridge and down the steep bank. Denis slid the canoe into the water and unlashed the paddles, while Lenora held firmly onto the stern painter. She could feel the water tug at the boat. The live feeling came right up the rope into her hands, and she felt as she had when she was catching the trout. Her mouth was dry and she kept licking her lips. An adventure at last!

"Okay, I'll take the painter. Hop into the bow and be ready to paddle as soon as I say."

Lenora walked carefully down the centre of the canoe, feeling it bounce and sway beneath her, and knelt in the bow, her back against the front thwart. Her right hand circled the stem of the paddle, her left firmly grasped the butt. She heard the scrunch of pebbles against the aluminum bottom, felt the canoe dip and sway as Denis climbed aboard. Almost before his rather breathless okay, she was ready.

She had never paddled on a river this fast, she realized, amazed at the power of the water against her paddle. She dug in fiercely.

"Don't work so hard." Denis's yell came to her above the sound of the water. "Just keep her nose in the current, and keep your eyes peeled for rocks and logs."

"Okay." She spread her knees apart on the bottom for better balance and peered ahead. The river was running due north at this point, with the sun flickering through the trees to her right, so that they paddled alternately through stretches of dark water and stretches that were spangled with gold. The banks — they were almost cliffs — on either side were of reddish-black shale with occasional shingle bars at the bottom that stretched out into the water.

For the first moment or so she was stiff with fear, fear that she would do something wrong, that she had been stupid to persuade Denis to go along on this wild excursion. But the canoe rode well in the water. She found it wasn't difficult to keep the bow right into the current, and though the water was very fast it seemed safe enough. No tricks. She began to enjoy herself. It was easy to see a rock by the white shine of its back wave, and she was usually able to anticipate Denis's shouts of left or right. They were a good team.

They had gone about one kilometre downstream when trees loomed up ahead and the river unexpectedly turned left, back towards the mountains. Easier to see, she thought, with the sun behind them instead of dazzling on the water. But...

"Hang on!" Denis's shout was panicky, as if what lay ahead was something he hadn't expected.

"Wow!" Lenora stared at the expanse of seething white.

"Left, left," he yelled, and she pried furiously to make the bow swing left. She was not quite quick enough or strong enough, and a smooth, waist-high wave slopped into the canoe. She gasped. It was as if someone had thrown a whole bucket of icy water over her. It soaked her T-shirt and shorts and swirled about in the bottom of the canoe. She gritted her teeth and paddled on.

Somehow they got through and into a comparatively calm stretch.

"You okay?"

"Sure. That was great, fabulous. I've never..."

"I didn't know there were going to be standing waves. Not that size. I must have read the wrong page of the guide."

He can't panic, she thought. *He's in charge.* "Have you got a bailer?" she shouted.

"Yeah. Tied to the stern. Think you can handle the canoe alone while I get this water out?" He sounded better.

"Sure I can." She clenched her teeth and squinted at the water. It was hard to know exactly what to do. It was all happening so fast. The important thing, she remembered from long-ago lessons, was not to let the canoe swing away from the current. If it did, there was nothing to stop the water coming in, and then...

"Help! There's another set of rapids coming up," she yelled. "Right or left? Quickly, Denis."

"I don't know. Right, I think. Yes, right. This is *crazy*. We should be ashore checking each stretch before going down. Only we can't, not here."

"It's okay, Denis. It's great."

They negotiated the fast water safely, though the last standing wave slopped clean over their bow. The water was like a wall, an ice-cold wall hitting her. There was water running down her face and hair. Into her eyes. She blinked and shook her hair back and went on paddling. "Are we all right, Denis? Are we going to swamp?"

"No, it's okay. We're through. Now comes the bit I read about. The easy bit. What an idiot..." She could hear him muttering to himself and she shot a quick look over her shoulder. He was bailing like mad, hurling the water back where it belonged.

The river was widening and slowing down from its frantic pace to merely very fast. She guessed that from their position in midstream to the shore must be about fifty metres, the same distance as the length of the swimming pool back home. That made the river about a hundred metres wide.

She looked down, but couldn't see the bottom. That was natural, of course. At the clip they were going it would be hard to see. But there was certainly enough water for rocks not to be a hazard. She kept a lookout anyhow.

The canoe moved beneath her knees as if it were alive; she found herself remembering the trick of keeping her body steady and upright, no matter how the canoe tossed or twisted. It was like riding a mustang bareback. It was like the wildest roller-coaster ride in the world. It was like... She began to sing at the top of her voice: "She'll be coming round the mountain when she comes..."

They paddled on. The river bent eastward, then changed its mind and turned north, then once more turned west. Then back to north. Without the sun to tell them what was going on, they would be in a complete muddle. How had the early explorers known where on earth they were going and what they were doing?

The trees, mostly spruce and pine, crowded the high banks. Now the sun was behind them, warming her wet shoulders. Ugh, there was nothing as horrid as a wet T-shirt clinging to the skin. She was lucky her life jacket had taken most of the splash.

Once more they turned east, and now the river seemed to change character. Its voice was subtly different. The banks were becoming lower. It ran straight ahead for a couple of kilometres. And then... She squinted her eyes. "It's an island, I think, Denis. I can't see anything but trees. Which side should we take?"

Denis concentrated on the memory of the map in his head. "The right side, I think. It turns south after the island, so the right side should be slower and give us a bit more time to make up our minds. If it's awful we can try to get ashore."

They paddled along a green passage that smelled of spruce gum, the low island to their left, the shore to their right. All the energy of the river had gone, concentrated on the northern side. It was a moment of peace, like on the quiet Quebec lakes she was used to.

Then the island was behind them, the width of the river ahead turning south, turning into sunshine. Ahead of them was the expected white flurry of fast water. Something else, before the white water began. A stretch as smooth as a silk sheet. Smooth and dark.

"Denis!" Lenora screamed, as she suddenly saw the ledge over which the silky water poured.

"I see it. Too late to go back. Keep going. Don't stop paddling whatever you do. And lean *back* as we go over."

They were being pulled into the centre of the smoothness. Lenora could feel the water tug at her paddle, nearly pulling it out of her hand. She hung on, working furiously to keep their bow straight down the middle. Suddenly she was paddling air and there was nothing she could do. She could feel herself screaming, feel the tension in her throat, but she couldn't hear herself because of the thunder of the water.

Slam. They were over and she was paddling furiously in foamy water that had no body to it. No matter how hard she dug in, they were going nowhere. The water thundered behind them. *In another second we'll drift back right under the water. We'll be swamped and it'll all be over*.

Lenora paddled wildly and at last felt the pressure of water against the blade of her paddle. They were free of the undertow, back in the main current, careering downstream.

"Another ledge," she screamed. Her throat felt like sandpaper.

"You're doing great. Take it just like the last time."

This time they flew free of the foamy water beneath the falls and there was none of that helpless terror of being drawn back under the cascade. But there was no time to relax. Now they were on a winding, choppy stretch of water with a few fairly safe-looking rapids. Lenora kept her eyes on the water, realizing that it was *her* control that would get them into trouble or keep them out of it.

They smacked into a couple more standing waves and Denis had to bail them out. Soaking wet, water dripping from her hair, Lenora couldn't stop smiling. They'd done it and it had been great. "She'll be riding six white horses when she comes..." she sang.

The river turned south, a long stretch almost into the sun, with the cliffs falling away on either side, turning into low banks crowded with spruce, pine, and aspen. A different country. Before Denis called out, she was expecting his words.

"We've got to ease over to the right bank and get ashore before the river turns east again."

"Okay. We'll have to crab over or we'll get more water in."

"Right. Back-paddle when I tell you."

Lenora glanced at her watch. Eleven-twenty. The others would be turning back from the store about now, Mom stocked up on cigarettes. That world of cars and stores seemed a zillion light-years away from the racing river, the dark forest, and the still sky.

I wish it wasn't over, she thought. *It's the first day that I haven't thought about Dad and the times before he left. It's the first time since we moved that I've felt happy. Maybe now that I've proved myself, Harry and*

Brian will let me be part of their adventures. She could imagine them with two canoes atop the station wagon, exploring Alberta rivers, camping along the banks. Poor Mom, she didn't come into the picture. She'd be waiting for them at the other end, ready to pick them up and take them back for some home cooking. Tough on Mom. But she *did* choose to marry Harry.

As they edged closer to the right bank, the sun caught the shadows of the treetops. Spears of light and dark alternately jabbed at her eyeballs. Flick, flick, flick. She looked down at the water, but the reflections of the light were there. Flick, flick. Light and dark. Keep an eye peeled for rocks and logs. The light was dancing behind her eyes now. It was hard to see anything at all. Migraines are not triggered by light, she told herself firmly. Tension, the doctor had said. She certainly wasn't tense now. She was having a splendid time.

Would Harry be furious at what they'd done? She'd have to make sure to take all the blame, or Denis would really be in trouble, with both Harry and Brian on his case.

Flick, flick, flick. Their canoe moved quickly through the bars of light and shade. Were they going to be able to get free of the current and get ashore at the place Denis had chosen?

"It's smoother just ahead," Denis yelled. "Maybe we can back-paddle there and get over quickly. What do you see? Any problems?"

She leaned forward, blinking. The dazzle behind her eyes was worse. It was almost impossible to see any detail. Was that a riffle just upstream of the smooth patch a sign of something under the surface? Or just her eyes playing tricks? She said nothing. They were only about thirty metres from shore. Once in the shade, her eyes would stop playing tricks.

With no warning at all, the canoe, which had been moving at about twelve kilometres an hour, stopped dead. Lenora was thrown into the air. She had the oddest feeling that time had stopped. That she was flying. She found herself moving her arms the way one does in dreams of flying.

Smack. The water came up to meet her. It hit her along the full length of her front. Face, chest, belly, legs. She went under and fought her way up in a panic, struggling for air. She gasped, saw the light, told herself that she was all right. It couldn't be too deep. She'd whacked one shin on the bottom when she'd gone under. She was only about twenty-five metres from shore. Peanuts. She was a competitive swimmer and she was wearing a life jacket. *There was nothing to be scared of.*

As these thoughts raced through her head, her arms and legs were moving automatically. She kept her head up and tried to breathe regularly. In her ears was the echo of Denis's scream: *"Lenora!"* So he was all right.

She grabbed a small, precious mouthful of air and then the swamper waves got her. No good even thinking about getting to shore until she was through this stretch. All she could do was to keep enough oxygen in her lungs. And not get her head bashed in on the rocks. That was what she had to concentrate on. Just staying alive...

8

Monday morning

Fingers biting into his shoulder muscles. Foul breath fanning his neck. Isaac woke with a yell and tried to leap to his feet. Something smashed into the top of his head and he collapsed, seeing stars. *Jeez.* He held his ringing head and looked up. A cedar bough. Not jail then and that sordid cellmate with the rotten teeth.

He rubbed his hands over his face. That nightmare again. He'd yelled so loud the guard had come. There'd been a fuss, he'd had a chance to talk to a guy from legal aid or something, and he'd been transferred to the jail in the foothills. Like a miracle. No one made a move on him. No one even talked to him, no more than was necessary. Which was okay with him.

The place wasn't that bad, and the food was better than he'd had in a year. He could actually see the forest from his cell window. Peaceful. Until the trees started talking to him. Not out loud, so other people could hear, nothing crazy like that. Just in his head.

After lights out, they were the loudest. Bars didn't hold back the scent of pine and spruce. Nor the voices.

"Have you forgotten?"

"Come home where you belong."

"Remember the old stories?"

He used to lie wakeful in the dark, remembering

Grandmother's stories. Of Morning Star, who took a native bride back to the sky, to live happily with him until the day she grew curious, dug up the giant turnip, and saw through the hole her people far below. How she became so homesick that Morning Star let her go, giving her the sun dance as his gift to her people.

Stories of the spirit search, of the dances and the medicine bundles. One night there was a storm and he remembered Grandmother telling him of the fight between Thunderbird and Rattlesnake. She told him of a man who had been struck by lightning and became a great shaman, because he had been touched by the power of mighty Thunderbird.

As he lay wakeful, night after night, Grandmother's voice seemed to grow stronger, until he could hear her calling him from the forest, as clear as clear. Then jail became a torment and the only thing that mattered was to be free.

She was calling him now from somewhere a long way off. "I'm coming, Grandmother," he called back, and the sound of his voice startled him into the present. He looked dazedly around him. He wasn't in jail. Prison was the dream, and this, the forest, was reality. The straight trees, going on and on in every direction, barred the white man, not him. He knew their secrets. It was his place.

He sniffed the air. Cold. Another good day. A good day for what? For walking. Where? Something about Grandmother. His head wasn't working the way it should, kind of slow and stupid, slipping into the past and back again, muddling him. He cast his eyes around, trying to remember.

There, just beyond the low branches of the great cedar, was a long line scratched in the dirt, a straight line with a triangle point at its far end. An arrow. Had he drawn it? And why? What was the matter with his head?

An arrow. That was to point the way to someplace. Someplace he had to go. Yes, that was right. He fumbled with the laces of his boots, got to his feet, and lumbered off through the trees in the direction of the arrow. In less than twenty paces he came upon a grassy avenue, edged with aspens and saskatoon bushes. Then he remembered.

Long ago, in some other time, he had seen a map of this region of the forest. It had been criss-crossed with a fine diagonal network of dotted lines, drawn, most of them, as straight as if a ruler had been laid down across the country, though a few of them curved to join other roads and trails.

These were the fire roads and seismograph lines. These were the green highways back to his people. Whoever had scratched the arrow sign in the dirt knew what he was doing. He looked up to get his bearings from the flush of red in the east, then set out along the cut in a northeasterly direction.

Straight as a bee's path, straight as the crow's flight, the cut lay across the land, disregarding the contours. It was not like the trail he had followed for the past two days. That had been a walking trail, skirting the base of mountains, following the valleys and the natural course of the creeks. Isaac found himself climbing three hundred metres in order to descend three hundred metres an hour later. It didn't matter to him. He walked in a daze, not asking himself where he was going or why. The green path led and his feet followed obediently.

He came upon the road unexpectedly. His feet hit the hard clay surface and he blinked and looked around, wondering what it was. Then he heard a truck engine labouring along to his right, and his feet carried his body at top speed across the road and into the brush on the far side.

He lay in the grass until the camper had lumbered southward. Then he got to his feet and followed the cut again. Not long now, he found himself saying, and stopped. Not long till when? There was no answer to that one. It was a question without meaning. There was only the present moment. There was no other time.

Slowly, steadily, not noticing the pain in his knees or his shortness of breath, he climbed over the shoulder of a tree-clad hill and down the far side. The land around him was becoming flatter. There were small streams that had to be waded. Aspen was growing, pale green, among the darkness of spruce and pine.

Now there were open spaces, almost meadows, around him. The sky opened above him and he could feel the heat of the sun on his shoulders. Ahead of him gleamed the river, blue and white, wide and slow moving. He staggered down the bank onto the sandy beach, took off his boots and socks, and waded into the water. Its coldness was like a benediction.

The canoe had slammed into the hidden obstacle like a car crashing at full speed into a brick wall. It stopped, shuddered, and overturned.

I should have been in the bow, Denis had time to think. *Stupid, stupid!* He saw a flurry of colour amid the white water, yelled "Lenora," and went under, choking.

Darkness all around. The overturned canoe above him. The weight of the water pressing him against the underwater obstacle. He couldn't move. He was in a nightmare of drowning, of being trapped and drowning.

A *strainer*, that's what it was. A drifting log, jammed against something, its branches catching every passing obstacle until it was like a mesh, letting the water through, but nothing solid. He could be pinned against these underwater branches until there was no more oxygen, until his brain stopped working.

No! He kicked furiously to try to free himself from the current, and felt an ankle caught and held in a spiky grip. Now the blood was pounding in his ears. He groped blindly with both arms, felt the frame of the canoe above him like a canopy, and kicked his foot free. With his last vestige of energy he pulled his knees to his chest, forced himself against the current, and straightened like a spring.

His body drove upstream, the life jacket popped him to the surface, and the current at once caught him again and smacked him against the hull of the canoe. Light and air. The bliss of breathing again, each indrawn breath a groan and a cough. He hung on desperately to the smooth hull of the canoe on the upstream side, his fingers reaching for, grabbing, the one-centimetre strip of aluminum that was the keel.

The current was appallingly powerful. He could feel it sucking at his legs, pulling them back under the canoe. If he relaxed for a second the water would have him again. He hung on and inched his way upward until at last he was lying along the upturned bottom of the canoe.

That was better. Spread-eagled along its length, he coughed the rest of the water out of his lungs and got in a few good breaths before looking around. The river was about a hundred metres wide at this point, curving away to the east, to the left. The tree in which the canoe was caught must have jammed across the river between two rocks, just a bit to the south of the central current. The same amount of water would be going down, but with less than half the area to get through.

So it was much faster. The white waves at the bow and stern of the overturned canoe told him just how dangerously fast the current was.

He moved slowly, afraid that the canoe might tip at any moment, though it seemed firmly wedged enough. He looked all around. Where was Lenora? There was no sign of her in the stretch of river downstream that he could see. Was she out of sight beyond the bend? Was she free of the deathtrap from which he had escaped? He had this clear mental picture of yellow and red flying through the air, flying clear, before he was submerged.

In spite of his memory, he kept having to reassure himself. An irrational part of him wanted to dive under the canoe again, grope around in the darkness beneath and make sure that she wasn't...But she couldn't be. He had seen her thrown clear. He *had*.

She was downriver somewhere, God knows in what condition. And somehow he was going to have to get himself and the canoe to shore and then start looking for her. Or go back and get help. Or both.

Panic began to choke him, but he recognized it and made himself take slow, deep breaths, made his mind go blank. "One thing at a time," he told himself. "One thing at a time."

The bow was pointing to the near shore, maybe forty metres away or a bit less. But the painter secured to the bow was only six or seven metres long. Even if he could untie the wet stern painter and fasten it to the one in the bow, the two pieces of rope still wouldn't reach the shore. So hauling the canoe ashore wouldn't work. Anyway, the paddles were gone, trapped underwater in the log jam or maybe floating downstream, kilometres away by now. So he'd better forget about the canoe and concentrate on getting himself ashore.

He wriggled as close to the bow as he could and began to study the current, planning his moves. As far as he could see, the tree didn't extend past the bow of the canoe, which was caught on the same rock that held the tree. If he jumped clear, he should be in no danger from its underwater branches.

Beyond the jam was a clear passage about six metres wide, and beyond that a scatter of visible rocks, challenging for a canoe, fierce for a swimmer. Maybe, if the current wasn't too powerful, if it didn't smash him against the rocks and knock him out, he might be able to scramble up and jump from one to another as if they were stepping stones, until he reached the clear water next to the bank.

The only catch was that, at this point, the river was turning east, so that the bank he had to reach was the outer one of the curve, the one where the current was going to be the fastest, since it had the greater distance to travel. A nasty-looking patch of standing waves made a barrier between him and the rock garden. If they swamped him and he couldn't reach the rocks, he was likely to be shot downstream for kilometres before he'd get another chance to get ashore.

No good hanging around, he told himself. He was cold and very tired and he hadn't even started. Better not to hang around any longer, getting colder and more afraid every minute. He gathered his body under him like a spring, crouched at the bow of the overturned canoe, and shot himself forward, pushing as hard as he could with his legs, stroking with his arms, sucking in air while he had the chance.

He aimed at an angle to the shore, an angle to the standing waves. The first one was okay and he got over it like riding the surf in Hawaii. But there was no time to get ready for the next one, and it smashed over his head, smothering him. Somehow he flailed through it, spluttering and gasping, not really swimming at all. By the time he'd caught his breath he'd nearly missed the rock garden. He crashed into the very last rock, bruising his right knee agonizingly. But at least he'd made it.

He clung to the smooth wet rock with his fingertips, and after he got his breath he launched himself across the foaming gap to the next rock upstream. There was no way of climbing on them, he realized; all he could do was fling himself across the gap from rock to rock, hang on until he'd caught his breath, and then go through the whole process again.

By the time he reached the far side of the scatter of rocks, he had made some progress back upstream and there was now only a narrow channel, no more than ten metres wide, between him and the shore. He hung onto the last rock and let his feet down cautiously. His runners just touched what felt like a pebbly bottom before his legs were swept out from under him by the current.

No walking ashore, then. The bank wasn't particularly welcoming at this point either. Rocky, with nothing much to hang onto and haul himself up by. *Wish I were a better swimmer*, he thought. *Like Lenora. Where is Lenora?*

He pushed himself away from the last rock and flailed across the river. The current ran smooth and dark. He gained a metre and no more. No matter how hard he swam he was being pulled downriver.

For just a second he relaxed and let the current take him along. Boy, was that fast! Once more he began to fight to gain the bank, a grudging centimetre at a time, but it wasn't until the river turned abruptly north again, about a kilometre farther downstream, that he was able to get close to the shore, to feel his feet securely on the pebbles, and stand up. He fell again and, on hands and knees, dragged himself ashore.

By now he was colder and more tired than he had ever been in his whole life. The effort of pulling himself up onto the bank seemed to have sucked the last particle of energy out of his body. He lay full-length on the grass, his eyes shut, gasping for breath.

Lenora. I've got to find Lenora. The thought goaded him back to his knees and then to his feet. He stared at the next reach of river. The sun was due south, shining on the water and the far bank. He could see along the bank for maybe a kilometre before it turned again. He looked hopefully for a figure in yellow and white, running towards him. He could imagine them hugging, feeling her aliveness. He longed for it, made it real in his mind.

But there was nothing. His eyes searched the scatter of jetsam along the shore for a person lying, maybe unconscious. Maybe... *No!* He pushed the thought out of his mind. She was a terrific swimmer. He'd seen the trophies she'd won back in Toronto. She'd make it. She *had* to. Because if she hadn't, then he, Denis Mathieson, was a murderer.

Last of all, hoping he wouldn't see it, he searched for an alien touch of colour, a glimpse of yellow or red or white, just below the surface of the water, caught in an eddy, snagged against a rock or another log jam. He made himself look twice, but there was nothing. He leaned against a tree, so thankful that he nearly passed out. He could hear the blood drumming in his ears, and his eyes went dark. When his head cleared he began to walk downstream, calling her name and looking along the shore, in the water, calling again and again. "Lenora. Lenora!"

When he heard a response it was like a miracle. He felt like throwing himself on the ground and thanking God that he wasn't a murderer, that she was still alive.

He called again and listened, his heart pounding. This time the answer was clear, the unmistakable raucous cry of a crow. Was that what he'd heard before? Had the damn bird fooled him? He called "Lenora" again and again. Each time, like an echo, the bird cawed back.

What in *heck* was he going to do? He had reached the point where the river was turning east in a definite and business-like fashion. The water was still a bit choppy. There were no eddies where a body might surface and float. There was nothing along the shore as far as he could see. And every metre was putting more distance between him and the camp.

He looked at his watch. 12:16...if it was still going. 12:17. Yes, it was. If he remembered the map, it must be nearly three kilometres back through the bush to the camp. The best part of an hour's slog. More, if the terrain was difficult. Dad and Brian would already be back by the time he got there. Wondering where they'd got to. And Hazel. Lenora's mother. He was going to have to face her. Tell her what he'd done.

I can't, he thought in panic. *I knew it was wrong. And dumb.* Sneaking a look at the guidebook in the middle of the night. *I misread it totally,* he realized. *There must have been a paragraph on the previous page. Something I missed. I'd never have taken a beginner on that water if I'd known what it was like. Jeez, I'm a beginner myself. What am I talking about?*

All right. Back to camp. As fast as I can. He half ran, half walked along the beach until he was back at the log jam. The canoe still lay across the river, wedged against the log by the current and maybe some boughs caught underneath. It marked the spot clearly, a green bar across the white water.

He dithered again, suddenly terrified that he had been mistaken, that maybe all this time Lenora had been trapped beneath the canoe. That he should have risked going back under to check.

The terror of the darkness, of the water pressing him against the branches beneath the canoe, the horror of being trapped, swept over him and he broke into a sweat. I *did* see her thrown clear, he told himself. I *know* I did.

He had to force himself to turn his back on the river. To walk away into the bush. West, with a bit of south in it, he told himself. He kept the sun in front of his left shoulder and tried to walk in as straight a line as possible, so as not to waste precious time.

He had been freezing when he crawled out of the river, but before long the sweat was running down his face. He stopped long enough to take off his life jacket. That was much better. Removing the bulky thing seemed to give him new energy.

But stopping, even for a minute, had given the mosquitoes a chance to catch up with him. They arrived in clouds and whined infuriatingly around his face and neck, biting him even through his shirt and jeans. At first he swatted at them furiously, but he soon realized that he was just wasting energy. He had to concentrate on getting back to the road, to the camp. He let them land and bite and only brushed them away when they settled near his eyes or mouth.

The bush here was mostly thick-set lodgepole pines, not easy to get through; and walking in wet runners wasn't the best thing in the world. There were dead-falls, spiky branches to tear at his ankles, roots to catch him unawares and send him stumbling headlong. He longed for a pair of good boots so he could really get over the ground.

He got his second wind and climbed steadily. He must be near the road. It was getting lighter ahead. And he could hear voices. Over to the right. He plunged through the trees towards them. He couldn't hear who it was, but *voices*. Someone who could help. He began to run. Broke out of the trees into the familiar clearing.

The store at Robb was small and it didn't stock Hazel's brand of cigarettes.

"There's not much difference, from the point of view of damage to your heart and lungs. But actually…" Harry picked the despised substitute off the counter. "…actually this brand is marginally less harmful than the ones you usually smoke."

"They also don't taste as good. Oh, well, I suppose they'll have to do.' She threw a twenty-dollar bill down on the counter.

Harry sighed and turned away. "Coming, Brian?"

"Just a minute, Dad. There's some little flies over here that aren't bad. Come and have a look."

Hazel picked up her change, ripped open the carton, and pulled out a package. "The ones over here are pretty noticeable, too," she said sarcastically, swatting at her arm.

"Hazel, didn't you say you wanted to see some fishing gear?"

"I've changed my mind. Thanks." She felt unaccountably jumpy. The stuffy little shop was stifling her. She pushed open the screen door and went out. The hand that lit her cigarette was shaking. *What's the matter with me?* She leaned back against the building and looked up at the incredible blue of the sky. She inhaled deeply and felt the tingle through her body. That was better.

The week wasn't going even half as well as she'd hoped. What *had* she hoped for? An instant family, coming together like iron filings to a magnet? A bit naïve, perhaps. But at least Lenora had stopped sulking.

Denis seemed to have taken a bit of a shine to her. That was okay. No harm in it. But would she ever get on with Harry and Brian?

Had she made a mistake marrying Harry? She tried to push the thought out of her head. The problem with making a mistake with one marriage was that one began to distrust one's own sense of judgement. She had to hang on to the memory of that instinctive feeling when she had first met Harry. That here at last was someone steady and secure. Someone who could be trusted not to throw over a job for a dream, or wipe out the family's vacation savings on a save-the-whales campaign. Someone who knew how to cope with a stopped sink or a broken refrigerator.

I suppose I could have gone on managing by myself. But that was it, when you came down to the bottom line...loneliness. She had had all she could stomach of loneliness. And Harry had been there, available and willing.

It was tough on the kids, having to adapt to each other. But she was thirty-eight. Nearly at the dread forties. Lenora would survive. In five or six years they'd all be grown up and living their own lives. It would have been stupid to have sacrificed her own life for Lenora.

But the guilt nagged at her...under the surface, like an almost-forgotten sore tooth, with just a jolt now and then to remind her that it was still there.

Harry and Brian came out of the store. "Sorry to keep you waiting, Hazel. Oh, do you want to finish that thing before we start back?"

"No, it's all right." He sure knew how to get the message of disapproval across, she thought, resentfully grinding her cigarette into the dirt, twisting her heel until the paper disintegrated and the shreds of tobacco were lost on the brown ground.

"You *do* understand I'm only thinking of your health, my dear. Statistics show clearly…"

If he had just kept quiet, she could have coped. She told him what he could do with his statistics, using a word that startled even herself. Harry did a double take and Brian went red. The journey back to the camp on the Brazeau River was silent.

I suppose I should apologize, thought Hazel. *But on the other hand, why should I? It's my business if I smoke. I'm damned if I'm going to let him start making me over into what he sees as a perfect wife.* She found herself wondering, not for the first time, what Harry's first wife had *really* been like. Her memory had been enshrined in portraits and photographs around the house, though Harry had tactfully put all of them out of sight after the wedding. All but two, which were permanent fixtures on the dining-room wall.

It's not fair, she thought. *When you're dead you have the last word. If Harry had been divorced, our marriage would have started out on a different footing. We would both have been in the same boat, two people who'd made a mistake and were trying to do it better the second time around.* As it stood, she was the only person who hadn't made it work.

It was about 12:30 when they crossed the Brazeau River and drove up the road to the campsite. Brian jumped out of the car and held the door open for Hazel. He was always careful about these little politenesses, but she had an uneasy feeling he was laughing at her. She nodded her thanks and took the carton of cigarettes into her tent.

The first thing she saw, lying against the wall by her sleeping bag, was the carton of her favourites, the ones she was so sure she had brought from Edmonton.

I mustn't let Harry see. He'd be furious. She tucked

them furtively out of sight and came out of the tent. *But I'm sure I looked there. I must be going crazy.*

"Denis! Nora!" Brian was shouting lustily. "Well, it would have been a kind thought on their part to have made lunch. I guess we'll have to go ahead without them. I'm starving, I don't know about you. What'll it be?"

"I'm not really hungry, thanks." Hazel lit another cigarette. "But I'd kill for a cup of tea."

"What about you, Dad?"

"Huh? Oh, anything simple." Harry was standing with his hands in his pockets, rocking from heel to toe, which he only did when he was furious. This was as far as he would ever allow his anger to go.

"Since I'm elected chef, do I hear anyone volunteering to pump water? No? Oh, well…" Brian took the battered camp kettle and went over to the pump to fill it. By the time he'd brought back the water and had lit the Coleman, the two of them were standing at opposite sides of their camp like two resentful sentinels.

With any sort of luck, he thought cheerfully, *this week'll see the end of this marriage.* The beginning of the end, anyway. The trip to Robb seemed to have brought things to a head nicely. He could certainly see the cracks in the foundation. He whistled as he cut bread.

"Sandwiches?" Brian waited until Dad acknowledged him with a grunted, "Sure."

"What'll it be then? Spam? Eggs? Peanut butter?… Buffalo chips?"

Harry and Hazel made vague assenting noises and he grinned as he got the food out of the cooler and began to butter bread. He shook out the tablecloth and spread it with a gesture over the picnic table before putting out the mugs and the plateful of sandwiches.

"Madame et monsieur, luncheon is served."

They ignored him.

"Oh, come on, you two! Grub's ready. *I'm* going to eat, anyway, and I warn you, this is the last and only lunch I'm making today."

Hazel blinked as if she were coming back from a long way off. She dropped her cigarette and ground it out. It had smouldered right down to the stub anyway, Brian noticed. In another second or two it would have burned her fingers.

She looked around. "Where *can* they have got to? Denis and Lenora?"

"I do know who you mean," Brian said. "I imagine they're fishing or exploring a trail."

"But it's one o'clock. Harry, the kids aren't back *yet*. Suppose something's happened to them…"

"Eat first," Brian advised with his mouth full. "And drink this tea before it's stewed."

"Well, I suppose…" Hazel looked around the sunlit glade. It all looked very safe and ordinary, downright cosy, in fact, with the red and white checked tablecloth and the matching mugs and plates. It was beyond the glade, where the trees took over, that it was frightening. Crowding together, thousands and millions of them. Uncountable trees going on and on in every direction. All exactly alike. Completely different from the fat, comfortable Ontario maples.

"They could have got lost," she said weakly, as she sat down at the picnic bench and took the mug of tea Brian passed her.

"Denis may be a bit of an ass, Hazel," Brian said condescendingly. "But he does know how to behave in the bush. I'm sure he won't let them get lost."

"For heaven's sake, Hazel, stop fussing. We've wasted a morning already. Let's at least have our lunch in peace and quiet. When the kids get hungry they'll come for food. It's as simple as that."

"If you're sure. But it's not like Lenora..."

"Come on. Try a sandwich." Brian passed the plate. "Spam with french mustard and alfalfa sprouts. More tea?"

You could strike sparks off the pair of them, he thought, as he munched. *But it is odd, Nora and Denis being away this long.* He sneaked a look at his watch. Harry caught the gesture.

"What's the time?"

"Not long after one."

"Why don't you go up to the bridge and do a recce?"

"Why don't I do that?" He unwound his long legs from around the picnic-table supports and strolled up the road, his hands in his pockets.

"Something *is* wrong. I just know it." Hazel fingered her cigarette pack.

"Nonsense. All your imagination." But Harry also got to his feet, prowled around the tents, looked at the perimeter of their camp. "Too bad there's no one else camping up here. Someone to ask. Someone who might have seen them."

Hazel shivered. "It's so damn quiet. So lonely."

They heard Brian's whistle and turned to see him jogging along the road from the bridge. "They're not up the river. Not within shouting distance, anyway. I wonder if they took any of the fishing gear."

"Two of the rods are gone." Harry poked around in the tent. "Denis's and my spare one. Damn cheek. They *must* have gone upriver, Brian."

"They went the heck of a long way then. I really yelled."

"But..."

"Go look for yourself, Dad, if you don't believe me."

"I know something's wrong." Hazel twisted her hands together.

Brian stood in the middle of the campsite and slowly turned around. "There *is* something. Something I should have...Wait a minute! The canoe! It was in the underbrush right over there. And it's gone."

"Oh, my God, Denis wouldn't be such a fool!"

"What's the matter? Oh, Harry, what is it?"

"The silly ass. Showing off to Nora, I'll bet you, Dad. But he'll never make it. There's sixteen kilometres of class-three white water downstream of the bridge."

"Maybe he can handle it, Brian. I think he *could* handle it."

"With a novice along? Come on, Dad. Be realistic."

"What are you *talking* about?" Hazel interrupted, her voice high.

"Denis has taken Nora downriver through rapids that are classified for experts only," Brian said, quite concisely, he thought.

Hazel instantly turned a dirty grey colour.

"Easy, love." Harry put an arm round her. "Brian, you idiot!"

"She *did* ask."

"What are we going to do? Oh, Harry, what are we going to *do*?"

"We have to work out what *they* were planning to do. I can't believe that they were intending to make the whole trip downriver. They haven't taken their sleeping bags. Or food. Just the fishing gear."

"And two life jackets."

"Thank God they remembered *that*."

"Harry, we've got to *do* something."

"Take it easy, Hazel. We don't really know that..."

"She's my daughter, for God's sake!"

"And my son."

"Sorry, sorry." She rubbed her hands over her face and took a deep breath. "All right now. What do you think we ought to do?"

"Wait for another hour. If they haven't turned up by…say, two-thirty, I think we'll have to assume that something's gone wrong."

Waiting. Waiting was a terrifying experience. Thoughts battered around in Hazel's head so loudly that they took all her attention. Whenever she managed to push down the frantic fears within, the silence outside was even more terrifying. She groped for her packet of cigarettes. It felt unbelievably light. *I do smoke too much. Harry's right. If I hadn't made him take me to the store, this wouldn't have happened.*

I should never have trusted Lenora with Denis. What do I really know about him? What do I really know about Harry, come to think of it? He was there when I needed him: security and a boost to my downtrodden ego. What a reason for getting married!

Oh, God, please look after Lenora. Don't let anything awful happen to her. If you look after her, I'll do anything. I'll give up smoking. I'll be a better mother. I'll make this marriage work, I swear I will. If you'll only…

Harry and Brian were on their feet. What was it? What had they heard? She pushed her noisy thoughts away and listened. A panting, sobbing sound. And breaking twigs. She ran towards it.

Harry caught her arm. "Hold on. It might be a bear."

A bear! Just what we need right now. A bear!

"It's all right." Brian caught a glimpse of red among the trees. "It's them."

Hazel's knees gave way under her. Thankfulness flooded her whole body like a shower of warm sunlight. Then anger drove out the thankfulness. How could they have been so thoughtless? How *could* they?

Denis burst out of the trees. His shirt was torn and there were lines of blood among the stains of perspiration where brambles had caught his skin. His hair hung damp and dishevelled.

"Well, you're in trouble now, buster," said Brian cheerfully. "What made you do such an idiotic...?"

"Where's Lenora?" Hazel screamed.

Denis stared at her, his mouth open. Then a huge sob burst out of his body. "I don't know. I think I've drowned her."

9

Monday afternoon

Stay alive, that was it…forget about timed strokes and proper breathing…sucked under again, fight to the top…important to avoid an undertow…but what about falls — please, God, no falls, please…I've got a good life jacket. I'll be okay if I don't get knocked out… arms above my head to protect it…ouch, no, better feet first, like going down a chute…that's it. Not so scary if I pretend I'm just going down a chute…Water Wonderland. Five bucks will get you the thrill of your life…that's better. Not much control, but some… knees flexed a bit to take the shock of slamming into a rock…stroke with my hands just the way I did with my paddle…keep my feet heading into the current. Draw and pry, remember?

The current's slower now. Wonder if I can make it to shore? Roll over and look downstream…oh, God help me!…more white water ahead…turn again, feet first. But I am still alive. I'm conscious. I can survive this. I *will*.

Got through that stretch okay…I'm getting cold. So cold. Mountain water, they said…if it's not straight off the glacier it's the next best thing…how long can I keep going? Roll over again and take a look…gee, it's so fast. Too fast to get to shore…rocks everywhere.

No, there's a patch of standing waves…Go for them.
Headfirst. Like surf riding.

This life jacket is a nuisance. You can't dive through
the waves, it's too bulky…holds me back…I'd do better without it. I'd be streamlined…can I get it off?
Damn, everything's swollen with water. My hands are
so cold…

Can't feel my feet against the rocks…just the jar up
my spine when I hit. More waves…slap across my
face…choke. Can't breathe…How long is this white
water going on? Can't go on like this forever. Got to
slow down some time…What was I doing?…taking
off my life jacket? I must be crazy…it's the cold…the
cold's doing things to my brain.

The river's slowing down…I'm slowing down…what
am I doing coasting along on my back?…roll over and
get moving. Terrible stroke. Sloppy, coach'll blast me
for that…no chance in the national championships if I
don't do better than this. Why can't I reach the end?…
the longest pool…can't see the end. Keep going…can't
see the spectators, but I bet Mom's there cheering…
Caw-caw…there's Mom all right.

Don't let your face go under, stupid…come on,
keep your chin up. Breathe, you're not a water baby…
not yet…might be kind of nice at that…warm…stop
fighting it…float on and on. Not cold any more…not
anything any more…

Isaac stood stupidly in the water. What was that?

"Caw-caw. Caw-caw."

"Old crow, are you talking to me?" Isaac stumbled
out of the water and stood on the beach. The land was
moving up and down under him. The trees were shim-
mering, beginning to turn around again in the old
sun-dance spin. He sat down abruptly.

"Caw-caw."

"I hear you, old crow. Are you calling me?" He staggered to his feet again. The axe hung at the end of his right arm like an appendage. Like part of him. He felt awkward and off-balance if he walked without it. Again the world did its sun-dance spin around his head. He grabbed at a tree and swallowed a sudden bitterness in his throat. Just his stomach complaining again. *Give the spirit a chance, stomach. Let the spirit speak.*

"Caw-caw."

"All right. I'm coming, old crow. Though I can't believe you're my spirit. That would be some joke on me. Old man playing games with Isaac."

He started to walk upriver along the bank and stubbed a bare toe painfully on a rock. He looked down at his brown feet, the toes swollen from all that walking, now wrinkled from the cold water. He had boots somewhere, didn't he? And socks?

He found them scattered in the grass and sat down and slowly put them back on. He did up the laces with slow, laborious care. Then he stood and looked around. The beach below the bank was shingled with water-smoothed pebbles. To his right the river wound among sandbars, shallow and quiet near the edge, more urgent in the deeper channels farther out. Between him and the next bend there was only the river, the beach, and the trees. A plover ran anxiously to and fro on stiff-kneed, stilt-like legs.

To his left the river narrowed. He could see quite a stretch along it. There was nothing and no one in sight.

"Caw-caw." An untidy black shape tumbled out of the sky like a clown. Then another. He began to walk upstream towards them. His feet did not feel the roughness of the shingle. He did not notice the sun shining on him, though he felt vaguely warm and comforted, without knowing why. He felt as if he were in a dream. His body was hardly there at all.

What was beginning to happen was like the telling of a story, something that had already happened a long time ago. He was prepared for anything. Or for nothing. So he wasn't in the least surprised or distressed when he almost stumbled over the body of a young girl, lying half in the water, half on a sandbar.

She was dressed in white and yellow and red. Sun colours. Above his head the startled crows called and tumbled in the air like the black cinders of a fire.

He knelt down and touched her shoulder with his left hand, the axe still tightly gripped in his right. Soaking wet. River wet. And cold. That made no sense. A child of the sun should be warm and dry. He tugged at the bulky red jacket and she rolled over onto her back. Yellow hair, yellow like the sun, streaked like weeds across her white face. A bump on her forehead, blue at its edges. Her eyes were closed.

He touched her cheek. It was as cold as winter. What did it mean? She had been sent to him, there was no doubt about that. The crows had been her messengers. Yellow, red, and white: a sun child. But a cold sun child? What kind of sign was that?

He stood up, his arms dangling at his sides, and felt the comforting heft of the axe in his right hand. He looked down at it. The sun flashed off the edge of the blade. That had happened before, a long time ago. And he had asked the sun for...for what? He searched his memory, but it had gone. Axe. Wood. Fire. Yes, that was what had to be done. He must make a fire and bring sun warmth back to the sun child.

With a new certainty, he looked around. A strip of dry shingle. Deadfalls. An uprooted tree for shelter against the wind. He chopped wood, gathered splinters, made a starter with the dry inside bark, which he frayed, then moulded into a round, soft ball. There was an almost frantic happiness inside him that made him want to dance and sing.

He felt in his shirt pocket for the matches that his fingers knew would be there, though his mind didn't remember why. The little flame caught the ball of frayed bark. It ate up the splinters he fed it. The fire wrapped its golden flames around the larger logs. The heart of it began to glow sun-red. He put the axe down carefully on a flat stone close to the fire and went down the beach again for the sun child.

She didn't weigh much — her bones were bird thin — but his knees sagged as he carried her up to the fire. What was wrong with him? He could vaguely remember being strong. Now he was as weak as a child.

When he laid her down close to the fire, her head flopped against the shingle. After thinking about it for a while he undid the soaked straps of her red jacket, took it off, and tucked it under her head. That was better. Then he stripped off his shirt and laid it over her body.

Heat shimmered in the air above the fire and was reflected off the hollow place where the tree had been uprooted. She lay in a pool of heat. That was good. He felt her hands, limp and icy. He began to rub them, one at a time, his hands moving instinctively from the fingers up the arms towards the heart. Then he took off her shoes and socks — one shoe, there was only one — and rubbed her feet and legs in the same way. He went on doing this for some time, alternating arms and legs, until at last it seemed to him that he could see some pinkness under the skin. Or was it just the reflection of the firelight?

After a long time she sighed, coughed, and turned her head. What should he do now? Food and drink to welcome the returning spirit. But what food? What drink? He had nothing at all. He remembered vaguely that he had not eaten or drunk anything for a long time.

He looked around. Even in the wilderness there were odds and ends that might be useful. He did not have far to go along the beach before he found a rusted soup can, a plastic bottle with its top cut off, and a length of tangled fishing line.

He scooped the plastic bottle full of water, brought everything back to the fire, and carefully detached the ragged top of the soup can before pouring water into it. Set down at the edge of the hot embers, it would not take long to boil. Then he climbed the bank and began to pick saskatoon berries. In ten minutes or so the plastic bottle was full of them. He found a large leaf and set it on a stone next to the sleeping sun child, then piled some berries on it.

What else could he do? The fishing line was a sign. Perhaps she might have brought a gift. He leaned over her, hesitating. Her eyes were still shut, but her cheeks were pink now and there was a fine dew of perspiration on her forehead. Her hair was drying to a mass of fine gold threads, like the sun when it filtered through the trees.

Her white T-shirt had two buttoned pockets. He opened them and felt carefully inside. A block of brown stuff that had once been wrapped in paper, paper that was now wet and dissolving. He sniffed at it and saliva filled his mouth. Chocolate!

He broke the bar into pieces and dropped them into the hot water in the can; he found a clean stick and stirred the brew until the chocolate melted. Then he set the soup can carefully on a stone close to the fire to keep warm.

When he put his fingers into the second pocket something pricked them and he drew back his hand with a startled drawn-in breath. Like a snake bite. He looked fearfully at the small red spot on his finger, then tightened his lips and again put his fingers into the pocket. This time he pulled out a pair of fish hooks, fancy flies whose coloured feathers and bits of silky thread hid their wicked-looking hooks.

"Thank you, sun child," he said aloud, looking at the still figure by the fire. Then he squatted beyond the fire's heat and began patiently to unravel the snarl of fishing line he had found. His shadow had moved until it pointed far along the beach by the time he had disentangled the line and wound it around a stick.

He tied one of the flies to the free end, took off his boots and socks, and waded out past the sandbar to a rock, frilled with white foam, that seemed to overlook deeper water. Squatting in the golden evening sunlight, he paid out the line and let the current float it downstream, patiently pulling it in, winding it hand over hand onto the stick, and letting it out again. Over and over.

He felt a tremor, pulled back instinctively, and hooked his first trout. Playing it, hauling it cautiously ever closer to the stone where he crouched, he cut his fingers on the fine line. He felt them sting, but disregarded the pain. The fish was a gallant lively creature that fought him every centimetre of the way upriver to the rock where he knelt. If it had not been for his need he would have been happy to let it go. He nearly lost it at the last minute, but managed to hook a finger through its gill slit and throw it on the rock. A fine rainbow trout, its colours glistening in the sun before they began to fade into death. The sun child. And now the rainbow...

She lay in deep shadow by the fire; covered with his dark shirt, she was almost invisible until he was close enough to see the reflection of the red embers on her fair hair. For one heart-stopping instant he had thought that she had gone.

He bent over her, touched the roundness of the buffalo stone, still in the pocket of his shirt, covering her. That had been the first sign, hadn't it? Buffalo stone. No, the medicine lodge…he'd forgotten that. Sun child. And the rainbow colours of the trout. Good things come in fours, he remembered…

Clatter, clatter. He filleted the fish and laid it on a stone close to the heat of his smokeless fire.

Clatter, clatter. He raised his head. A long way off, an alien sound intruded on the single purpose that filled his head. He poked the fish a little closer to the embers.

Clatter, clatter. Close, fearsomely loud, almost overhead. Instinctively he leaped up the bank and rolled into the undergrowth, his heart thudding fearfully.

Was this another spirit visitation? Was Thunderbird angry that the sun child had come to him? What would Thunderbird do to him? He lay still with his head buried in the coarse grass, not daring to look up, hardly daring to breathe.

He could hear the fearsome noise. In his imagination he saw the creature beat its enormous wings. It moved upriver, away from him, away from the sun child. He let out his breath slowly, but lay motionless until the clattering noise had faded. Only when the forest was silent again did he raise his head.

The friendly crows cawed an all clear and he slid down the bank to the beach. She lay unmoving, though her lips and cheeks were pink. He touched her feet. They were warm. A sense of happiness and a heady kind of power flooded his body. It was all right. He was accepted. Safe from the all-seeing eyes of Thunderbird, he was safe from everything.

10

Monday afternoon

"Brian and I'll go down to the river. Walk along and see if we can spot anything." Harry had the map out, working out a route. "Hazel, you must drive back to the highway. Remember the forest-warden station? On the north side of the road back towards Rocky Mountain House — not far."

"But…"

"Denis'll go along so you don't lose your way. Are you all right? Can you manage that, Denis?"

"Of course I can, Dad. But I think I should drive. Hazel's too upset…"

"Nonsense. You don't have a licence, and, more to the point, you're not insured. Hazel'll be all right, won't you, dear?"

"I don't know. I think maybe…"

Harry pushed them into the car, slammed the door, picked up the first-aid kit and a bundle of blankets, and strode off into the bush with Brian, equally laden, at his heels.

Hazel told herself that Harry's control of situations was one of the things that had appealed to her. She got the key into the ignition at the second try, put the station wagon in gear, and instantly stalled it. She could feel her hands shaking and she clamped them hard on the wheel.

"It's okay. Try again," said Denis softly.

"Don't tell me how to…after all you've…" She choked on the words, jammed down the clutch, clashed the gears, and put her foot on the gas pedal. The wagon bounded off the grass onto the road.

A kilometre down the road there was a dip with a swampy bottom, a patch of pure gumbo. The wagon slid into the slimy stuff, slewed around, and stopped. Hazel bit her lip and swallowed. When she took her hands off the wheel, they wouldn't stop shaking. Denis said nothing.

"Go around, Denis," she said at last. "You're driving."

"But Dad said…"

"Do as I say."

Denis skirted the patch of mud and climbed into the driver's seat as Hazel slid over. He backed carefully away from the tree they were pointing at and got the car straightened out and on the road again.

After five minutes Hazel groped in her pocket for her cigarettes. "Can't you go any faster?"

"Not on this road. I'm doing the limit, honestly."

They passed the turn-off to Brown Creek camp. Denis glanced quickly at Hazel. Her face was hard, giving nothing away. Like stone.

"I…I'm awfully sorry."

"Words are easy. Oh, I'm sure you mean it, Denis. But *words*. Jozef — my ex-husband, you know — he was into words. Liked to call himself a 'wordsmith.' I think he felt it had a more effective, masculine sound than 'poet.' It was the only effective thing about him. I *despise* words."

"Lenora and I…we were getting to be really good friends, you know. She…"

"For God's sake, don't talk about her in the past like that. She's not…we don't know…"

"I didn't *mean* that. We *are* good friends. I meant we'd just started getting to know each other yesterday. The river trip was supposed to...she wanted...oh, heck, I suppose I just wanted to show I was every bit as good as Brian, that's all, really."

She didn't answer. He bit his lip. What had he expected? Absolution? Thank goodness, there was the highway ahead. He dived across the oncoming traffic and turned left up the road. Not far now.

The station was as neat as a cottage in a movie, the trim, freshly painted beds of petunias edged with dusty miller, the grass mowed to a velvet smoothness. The gardeners were still at it, one man raking the driveway, another on his knees weeding among the petunias, a third trimming the edges of the grass.

Denis stopped and ran around to open the door for Hazel, but she was up the steps and already pushing open the screen door before he got to her.

"My daughter...in some rapids..." she was saying as he followed her in and the screen door banged behind him.

"Where? Which river?"

Hazel turned to Denis. "*He* was there."

His face flamed at the scorn in her voice. "The Brazeau," he managed to stammer. "About ten kilometres downstream from the bridge, maybe a bit more."

"Canoe? Kayak?"

"Canoe, sir."

"You were together?"

"Yes, sir." Denis swallowed. He felt just as if he'd been put in the stocks and they were about to start throwing stones. "We hit a log jam and the canoe tipped. I got ashore. I looked everywhere for Lenora...I couldn't see..." *How the man must despise me,* he thought. *I should have stayed...gone on looking...*

"You did the right thing notifying us. We'll get a helicopter over the site right away. He'll see far more than you could hope to." He lifted the phone and talked quietly for a few minutes, then hung up and turned to Denis. "Right, then. He'll be off the ground in no time. Meanwhile, young man...what's your name?"

"Denis Mathieson."

"All right, Denis, show me on this map exactly where you were when the accident occurred. Then we'll take down all the necessary particulars."

The map was much bigger than Dad's, about one to fifty thousand. Denis could pick out right away the bend where they'd hit the log jam.

The warden glanced over at Hazel, who was walking restlessly up and down, smoking. He put his hand on Denis's arm and spoke quietly in his ear. "How certain are you that the girl — your sister, is it? — got free of the jam? Could she still be there? Under the canoe?"

Denis pulled his arm away. "Of *course* she was thrown free. I may be an awful idiot, but I wouldn't have left if there was any chance that she was still stuck underneath." His voice broke and he swallowed. "I can see it just as clear as...a patch of red and yellow flying through the air. As clear as I can see you right now."

Hazel turned. "What do you mean, Denis, red and yellow? Lenora wasn't wearing anything red today. You're making it up. Or you're dreaming. You never *did* see her. Oh, my God, she's probably trapped under the canoe this very minute, while we're wasting time...." She bit her knuckles.

"I swear I saw her. Red and yellow. Just a blur, before I went under. Then I was under the canoe, against the jam, fighting to get out. I know she was flung clear. I *know*. Red and yellow... Of course. The red life jacket! You see, Hazel, she *did* get out. I saw her life jacket and shorts."

They all turned as the door opened. A young man came in, not much older than Brian, in shorts and a T-shirt. "What's up, doc?" he asked cheerfully. "Another campfire out of control?"

"Canoe accident. On the Brazeau." The young man's face changed as he looked at the place the warden pointed out on the map.

"All right. I'll radio in as soon as I'm over the site."

"Will it be long?" Hazel interrupted.

"No time at all, ma'am. Try not to worry. I'll let you know as soon as I see anything."

The door slammed behind the pilot. Hazel was trembling all over now and Denis tried to put his arm around her, but she twitched away.

The warden got her into a chair and put a blanket around her. Then he brought her tea, hot and sweet, and made her drink it, though she protested feebly that she hated sugar. *I suppose he's used to this kind of crisis*, thought Denis, hovering uselessly around. *I wish I could do* something...

Hazel looked up from her cup. "Lenora's a very strong swimmer."

"That's good." The warden nodded, but Denis felt, with a sickening lurch, that he wasn't impressed.

"She'll be competing nationally next year, her coach says."

"And with a life jacket, she'd have every chance, ma'am. The fact that your son saw her flung free is the best possible news."

"He's *not* my son!" The warden looked startled and Denis flinched as if she'd reached out and slapped him. "I mean..." Denis flushed as she avoided looking at him. "I mean I just recently married Denis's father.

And Brian's...Lenora is my daughter by a previous marriage."

"Is your husband along on this trip?"

Denis interrupted. "Dad and my brother Brian went down to the river to see if they could find Lenora. They took blankets and...I *told* them I'd already gone downriver as far as the big bend after the spill. I don't think they believed me. I *did* look, though. I looked everywhere."

"I expect they just wanted to make sure."

"That's my dad. Has to see everything for himself." He tried to smile and failed.

The radio crackled in the next room and the warden went to answer it. Denis and Hazel listened tensely. It was maddening. They could hear the warden's questions, but not the pilot's answers.

He came back. "He's located the canoe. Still caught in the jam. Couple of men on the bank. That'll be your husband and stepson, ma'am. No sign of anyone else."

"She *must* be there. Maybe farther downriver?" Denis's voice faded.

"That's a good possibility. The problem is looking for her at this time of day. Right now the light on the river itself and the north bank is not bad, but much of the south bank is in deep shade. The pilot could see nothing, but that doesn't necessarily mean..."

"Then she could be anywhere...among all those dreadful trees. My poor baby. Suppose she tries to get back to camp?"

"I devoutly hope she'll have the sense to stick to the river bank. As soon as it's light tomorrow morning we'll start a full-scale search..."

"Not tonight? *Please*. You *can't* wait. All alone in the dark..."

"Hopeless. The men would just lose their way in the bush."

"But suppose she's hurt? Suppose..."

"First thing in the morning, the helicopter will be out again. The south bank will be in the sun for a while, if there's anything to see. And we'll have men out looking."

"What can *we* do to help?" Denis asked.

"I think the best thing would be to get back to your campsite. That's at the Brazeau River bridge? I hope your husband and son will be back there by the time you get there, ma'am. Tell them to sit tight. Don't let them wander around the bush at night. We'll just have more lost bodies to worry about. Would you prefer to come down and stay here until we have news?"

"No!" Hazel's voice was emphatic. "I want to be there. Close."

"Then I suggest you move your camp down to Brown Creek. There's a fire tower there. I'll be in touch with the lookout and he'll keep you informed."

"The lookout!" Denis stared. "Jeez, I blew it again. We could have stopped there and asked for help. Saved an hour."

"I don't think an hour would have made that much difference, son."

"That's funny." Hazel's laugh was bitter. "We were actually staying down at Brown Creek first. Lenora visited the lookout and got friendly with the young man. I wasn't happy about that. A total stranger. So I persuaded my husband to move on to the next site. If I hadn't done that, maybe this wouldn't have happened."

"You were worried about Pete? Oh, but he's a good lad. Anyway, I'll tell him to keep his eyes peeled. You never know. And he'll drop by and bring you up to date when I have any news."

"Couldn't I stay here and join a search party?"

"Are you experienced in the bush, son?"

"No, but I want to help. It was my fault."

"The best thing you can do is look after your step-mother and persuade your father and brother to sit tight and not take any risks themselves. And try not to worry, both of you. We'll do our best."

"You've been very kind." Hazel got up and walked out. The screen door slammed behind her.

Denis turned back. "Sir, what are her chances? Honestly."

The man hesitated. "Honestly? Hard to say. Even if she wasn't hit on the head going through that rock garden downstream of the jam, the odds on hypothermia are pretty high. But if she was still conscious and got ashore and was able to move around and keep warm, well, that's another story."

"The helicopter pilot was looking for a body, wasn't he?"

"Primarily. The fact that he didn't see a sign of her down the whole stretch of river — right down to the reservoir — well, that's a good sign as far as it goes."

"Thank you." Denis turned and pushed open the door blindly. Hazel was standing by the car, looking absently at the gardeners.

"How can they afford so much help? I thought the government was short of money."

"Oh, I guess they're guys from the jail."

He held the door open for her. She ignored it, staring back. "You mean, they're prisoners?"

"Sure. What's the matter, Hazel?"

"That first day at Brown Creek. Remember? The warden told us to be on the lookout for an escaped prisoner."

"Yes, so he did. I'd forgotten."

"With an axe!"

"What do you...? Oh, come on, Hazel, surely you don't imagine..." He tried to laugh. "That would be carrying coincidence a bit far, wouldn't it? D'you know how many hectares of forest there are in the Rocky-Clearwater Forest alone?"

"No, and I don't want to. Just the idea of my little girl alone in the forest with an escaped prisoner skulking around..." She shivered.

"Hazel, listen to me. An escapee would have set out at top speed for Edmonton or Calgary. Some big city where he could get lost, maybe connect with friends. He certainly wouldn't be drifting about in the forest. Not now. That was three days ago."

"You truly don't think I should worry about him?"

"Truly. He's long gone by now, if he was ever there."

11

Monday night and Tuesday morning

She woke with light in her eyes. *I must have overslept horribly*, she thought. *Perhaps that's why my head hurts so.* She turned restlessly, feeling her muscles ache. Did she have the flu? Her pillow felt as if it were stuffed with bricks, and something hard was digging into her hip. *What on earth...!*

She opened her eyes and found she was staring into a fire. A fire of logs and bleached driftwood, so close she could reach out a hand and touch it. So close to the fire, yet she was cold. Desperately cold. She shivered and drew her knees up to her chest.

"Welcome, sun child." The voice was not one she recognized. "If you will sit up I can put my shirt on you properly. You will be warmer then."

She sat up obediently, like a small child obeying a doctor, and felt hands push her arms through the sleeves of a shirt, felt gentle fingers do up the buttons. She stretched out her cold hands to the fire.

"You are missing your father, of course," the voice went on matter-of-factly. "But you will soon be warm. I have food and drink for you. *Hot* food and drink."

She could hear the pride and shyness in his voice, and she wasn't afraid. She turned towards him, but could see only a shadowed face, a bare torso, and legs clad in dark pants. He knelt beside her and, with as ceremonial an air as if it were a silver goblet, handed her a rusty tin can.

"What...?" She bent her head to the can and, improbably, smelled hot chocolate. She took a gulp. The warmth and the sugar brought a transfusion of energy into her cold body. She took another gulp. "Oh, that's good."

A log broke apart, and in the sudden flame that sprang up she saw his face for the first time. His cheeks were hollow, his lips dry and cracked, and in the black eyes she read hunger.

"Here." She held out the can.

"But it is for you."

"You too. Halves. I insist."

He took the can from her at once, held it up as if it were a holy thing, and then drained it. He sighed and she thought his face looked a little less pinched. As for herself, for some reason she was absolutely starving. When had she last eaten? And where? That was too difficult to puzzle out.

"Did you say you had food as well?"

He turned and showed her a flat stone close to the fire on which lay white fillets of freshly baked fish. Her mouth watered, and at his gesture of invitation she picked up a piece and stuffed it in her mouth. She could feel herself drooling and wiped a hand across her mouth. "Gosh, that's good."

She reached out for a second piece. He watched her, unmoving, sitting back on his heels. *Oh, what a pig I am*, she thought. "Hey, you too. Remember what I said. Halves."

The brown hand that reached for a piece of fish was trembling. His eyes closed for an instant as he put the food in his mouth. *How long since he's eaten?* she wondered. They ate, turn and turn about, until there wasn't a single flake of fish left on the stone.

She sighed. "That was absolutely terrific!"

"You are pleased?"

"Of course. It was a marvellous meal. I can't think how…"

"There are berries, as you know." Again the note of quiet pride in his voice. It was as if…as if she were the queen of this place and he was a subject. He showed her a big leaf, piled high with small purple berries. Again she had to force him to take half. They were a bit like blueberries, but more pippy. By the time she had eaten the last one, the shivering inside her stomach had gone.

"Are you well?"

"Terrific, thanks. I just feel enormously tired." She stifled a jaw-cracking yawn.

"Then sleep, sun child. I will watch and keep the fire going."

At this comforting suggestion she snuggled down with her head on the lumpy pillow. She had no questions. No fears. The fire crackled and her stomach felt comfortably full. She slept.

The next time she woke the moonlight was on her face. Her legs were freezing. She must have dropped the bedclothes onto the floor. She groped blindly and felt pebbles. With a jolt in her heart she sat up and saw the sky above, the moon floating bland and white, the trees a black, ragged line to her left. Over to her right a moving line of silver — could it be water? *Where on earth am I? What's going on?*

Close by, a glowing mound of wood, sifted over with white ash, glimmered in the shadows. She looked down at herself. Yellow shorts, bare legs and feet; no wonder she was freezing. On top, a too-large shirt that smelled in some way alien. Sweat and cedar gum. Not unpleasant. Just unfamiliar, like this whole scene. She felt as if she were in one of those old surrealist European movies that Dad used to like to take her to, movies with the kind of place where the trees might turn into stone archways or put out groping arms and hands.

She shivered. It was incredibly quiet, this strange place. She had a feeling that the world she had been expecting, that she couldn't quite remember, was a great deal noisier than this one. The only sound was a whisper from the water over to her right. No, it wasn't! There was another sound. She strained her ears and held her breath. It was a soft, even sound. Very close. Or so it seemed. The sound of something breathing.

Bears. The word jumped into her mind, she didn't know why. Someone had warned her about bears, not so very long ago. Only she couldn't remember who or why. She couldn't remember anything. It was infuriating. But there was the sense that out there something large and fierce was waiting for her. Breathing.

She put her knuckles in her mouth and bit down on them. *I won't scream*, she told herself. At that moment a log broke in half as the fire ate through to its heart. As its ends flew upward there was a sudden crackle and a shower of sparks. *Soon the fire will go out*, she thought. *Then whatever is breathing out there will come closer.*

She rose cautiously to her knees, then to her feet. In the faint light of moon and fire she could see a pile of wood, already chopped to size, lying in the shadow of the bank. She stooped to pick up an armload and saw the shadow just beyond turn solid. She almost screamed, but drew the sound back in a gasp.

It was all right. Not a bear. A man...more of a boy, really. He was lying curled on his side with his naked back to the fire. He must be freezing without a shirt, she thought. She looked down at herself, at the coarse, dark shirt she was wearing over her T-shirt and shorts. Thoughtfully she unbuttoned it, slipped it off, and laid it carefully over his body. Then she put wood on the embers, quietly, so as not to disturb his sleep, and went back to her place on the other side of the fire.

For the rest of the night she dozed uncomfortably, constantly aware of her freezing legs, of the incredible discomfort of her bumpy pillow, of the headache that throbbed behind her temples. When she put a hand up to her forehead she found a big hard lump. *Where did I get that? And when? No wonder my head aches. It must have hurt like mad at the time...what time? Why can't I remember banging my head? Why can't I remember what I'm doing out here? Who is that boy?*

She woke for the last time in the grey pre-dawn. She could hear sleepy bird sounds from the aspens that bordered the river. The fire crackled with fresh wood, smelling dry and sweet. She sat up and looked around. The boy had gone and she was alone.

She slipped away from the fire into the bushes. When she came out she went down to the river to wash. She saw him then, like a carved statue, kneeling on a rock in the stream. He did not seem to notice her and she said nothing to him.

Instead she went back and poked at the fire. It was a good hot blaze, a pity to waste. She looked around. It was really very odd that there seemed to be no camping gear, no utensils, not so much as a pan or a kettle. *I'd give anything for a good cup of tea. And bacon and eggs and hash browns.* The thought of food made her stomach growl and her mouth water.

Maybe he's stashed his tent and gear in the bushes. Maybe there's a rucksack full of food hidden somewhere. I could surprise him and make breakfast for us.

But though she scouted around, she could find nothing at all. Just a rusty soup can and a cut-off plastic bottle, the sort of thing people used for bailing out canoes... A memory stirred deep in her mind as she looked at it. What was it...on the tip of her mind?

In the end she washed out the soup can, filled it with river water, and set it close to the fire to boil. She sat close by, warming herself, and the water had just begun to bubble when she heard footsteps crunching on the pebbles behind her. She turned. "Hi!"

"Hello." He stood awkwardly, his head bent over the huge silvery fish with blue and gold markings that was cradled in his hands.

"Is that our breakfast?" She broke the silence.

"Yes. If it pleases you." He came out of his frozen pose, put the fish down on a rock, cut off its head with the axe, and cleverly used the edge of the blade to gut it. He wiped the axe blade on the grass, buried the head and guts neatly in the sand, and took the fish back to the river to wash it.

"It will bake in the fire," he said when he came back. "With herbs inside."

"Sounds delicious. I was going to make tea or coffee or something. But I couldn't find your gear. I boiled water, though..." She indicated the rusty can, expecting him to laugh and produce out of thin air one of those neat aluminum nests of cups and pans that solitary hikers use. But he didn't.

He nodded gravely, raked the fire aside, and set the big fish, propped up with sticks, against the hot embers. "You would like tea?"

"Yes, please. My head aches, though I don't know why. It's funny..."

Her voice trailed off as he climbed the bank, stooped and began to pick the small dark leaves growing there. "What's that you're picking?"

"Tea. My gift to you, sun child." He threw the leaves in the boiling water.

"Why do you call me that?"

He turned, surprised. "What?"

"Sun child. You keep calling me that."

"You do not wish to be known by that name? What shall I call you, then?"

"My name is...my name is..." Heavily, from the back of her mind, a sound lumbered up. "Lenora. Yes, that's it. Lenora."

"It is a beautiful name. What is its meaning?"

"It's kind of corny, really. My father was a poet and he chose it. Don't laugh. It means 'the Bright One.'"

"Yes, of course." He nodded and looked happy, as if she had just confirmed something he already knew about her.

But it's more than I know myself, she thought. *Though things are sneaking back, like my name and knowing what it means. Only who is this boy?* She had no recollection of him at all, not that that meant anything much. She seemed to have almost no recollections. Not even of the father who had chosen her name.

She took a good hard look at the boy as he bent over the fire to check the fish. His skin was bronzed, his eyes very dark, and his hair black and smooth, worn long and tied at the nape of his neck with a leather thong. Either he had a razor in his pocket or he hadn't begun to grow a beard. Above his smooth, hollow cheeks, the bones were very prominent. It was an interesting face.

His voice was light, with a faint accent that she couldn't place. She got the feeling that he talked to her in a special way, something more formal than his everyday speech. Why? Who was he and what was she to him?

He was a native, she realized. Was that why he was out in the bush with no gear? *Does anyone live like that nowadays?* she wondered. Surely not. Especially in the foothills, where the temperature could get close to zero in the middle of the night, even in August.

"Why don't you have a tent? Or pots and pans? Not even a knife?"

"As you know, Lenora, I came away with an axe. That is all I need. That and the gift from you."

"What do you mean, 'as I know'? I don't know anything about you. Or do I? I'm sorry. My head..." Her voice trailed off at his puzzled expression. "Did I give you a gift?"

He showed her a couple of fish hooks and memory stirred again. Someone's fish hooks — no, flies, that's what they were. Someone...

He was frowning, looking at her anxiously. She smiled and said, "Well, the gift comes right back with that delicious-smelling fish. Do you suppose it's ready yet? I'm starving, aren't you?"

He smiled, suddenly good-looking in a gaunt way, and pulled the fish away from the fire. He divided it into two parts, piled them on leaves, and offered her one. It was marvellous, blazing hot, flavoured with herbs, and most unfish-like. *I don't think I'll ever want to eat frozen slabs of something ever again, not after this,* she thought.

The tea, on the other hand, was an awful mistake. It was hot, but that was all. It reminded her of...herb teas, that was it. The year Mom decided that caffeine was bad for them. There was a miserable year of no tea or coffee, no Cokes, no chocolates. Then, like her other fads, it faded away and she had gone back to her cigarettes and endless cups of tea.

I remembered! Now she knew that on the other side of this nagging headache was a life full of memories. It was all right. It was coming back. If only she could put a face to the word "Mom."

Stop worrying, she told herself, and made herself relax and look around. The sun was just rising above the dark forest downriver. In the east, the few clouds near the horizon were flushed a brilliant pink. The rest of the sky had a pale, newly laundered look. It smelled clean, too. Fresh and sharp and tingly.

The river talked comfortably to itself in front of her, and at her back the fire was warm. Someone, not long ago, had said that the early morning was the best time of the day in Alberta. She could remember despising whoever it was at the time, but maybe he was right.

The native boy sat peacefully beside her. The silence was comfortable and she felt no need to fill it with talk. The light strengthened. The silence was suddenly broken by a faint fluttering sound.

She looked up. The sound was too regular to be anything but man-made. The sound grew louder. The boy leaped to his feet and kicked sand over the fire, scattering the embers. He grabbed his axe and the red life jacket in one hand and caught hold of her wrist with the other.

"Hey!" There was no time for further protest. He was strong, much stronger than she would have guessed, and he hauled her up the bank, through the rough grass and low brush, brush that scratched her bare legs, and into the dark chill of the trees.

"What are you doing? What's the..." Her protest was cut short by his hand over her mouth. Her back was pressed against a tree and he leaned against her, his shoulders wide, as if he wanted to hide her from view. His face was so close to hers that his breath fanned her cheek. His eyes were slewed to one side, looking back to the river. The whites of his eyes showed against his dark face.

She looked past him. It was a helicopter, beating slowly upriver. It was flying very low and it swayed slowly from side to side so that its tail seemed to wag. The sun caught the curve of the plastic bubble. The noise of its blades and engine was like thunder. Its wind whipped through the trees. She saw the boy's eyes close in terror and she fought against his hands, twisting her head from side to side.

She tried to lash out at his ankles, but her feet were bare and his were protected by heavy work boots. The thunder dwindled to a clatter, the clatter to a faint flutter. His face relaxed, and in that instant she pulled away from him and began to run towards the beach.

As if a curtain between the present and the past had been suddenly torn away, Lenora knew who she was and what had happened. She remembered the rapids, the sudden jolt, and the shock of cold water. The helicopter had been searching the river for *her*. For *them*. Had Denis been as lucky? Was he still alive? It was suddenly the most important thing in the world that Denis should still be part of it.

Oh, please let the helicopter come back! It was turning. The noise was louder. Deafening. Almost overhead. It whipped the aspens at the edge of the forest. One more stride and she would be in full view of the pilot. But, in that final step out into the open, her legs were tripped from under her and the ground came up and smacked her in the face.

She rolled into a ball and fought to get breath back into her body. By the time she was able to breathe again the river and the forest were quiet. She had missed her chance. She lay on her face and let the tears come.

"Don't cry. Please don't cry." The words were repeated over and over. "I had to hide you. Thunderbird is jealous. He would take you away from me. Back to the sun. He came before, looking for you."

She sat up and stared at him, wiping her wet face with the back of her hand. "What are you *talking* about? Are you crazy? That was a helicopter, looking for me. Thunderbird? Sun child? You *are* crazy!"

She shrank away and he caught her hand. "I worked so hard for you to come to me. I walked from the edge of the forest to the river. Three days and nights. I didn't eat or drink. Not a drop of water until you gave me permission. You can't leave me now. You're all I've got."

"But I'm not yours. I'm not anybody's. I'm myself. Lenora Rydz. Who are you, anyway?"

"You must know me. I danced the sun dance for you. I made a vow and fasted. I prayed to the Great Spirit. I did it all so you would come to me."

His eyes rolled to and fro, flashing in the morning light. His left hand opened and closed jerkily. His right hand was still. His right hand held the axe. Oh, God, the axe!

"I know who you are!" She scrambled to her feet. "You're the prisoner who escaped from the jail, aren't you? The warden warned us to look out for you. You just stay away from me. My father and brothers will be looking for me. They'll be here any time now..." How was she to get away?

To the river? What use was the river...she didn't have a canoe any more. And the helicopter was gone. *I must get back to Mom and Harry. To Denis and Brian. The marvellous ordinary everydayness of bickering and making up again. Back to camp.*

She slipped past him into the forest and began to run. The trees closed around her. They were like sentinels. Like prison bars. Once among them she could no longer see the sun, no longer guess which direction she should run in. Uphill, surely, back to the road. Running anywhere was better than staying. With that crazy guy. The guy with the axe.

She could hear him crashing through the undergrowth behind her and she kept running. But her feet were bare, and her stride was shorter than his. He caught up with her before she had gone fifty metres.

She screamed, but he paid no attention, just pulled her back to the beach. She sat on the sand, rubbing her bruised feet. She was shaking, but through her terror a small, logical voice spoke: *Be calm. Don't let him get mad at you. Try to persuade him to let you go.*

"Please. My parents…they'll be going crazy." She stumbled over the phrase, swallowed, and went on. "Denis and I were canoeing. Downriver from the Brazeau bridge, do you know it?" He stared at her, his dark eyes giving nothing away. "The canoe hit something and I was thrown out. The current was so strong it was all I could do to keep my head up. I don't know where I am, how far downriver. I don't know if Denis is okay or…My mother must be thinking I'm drowned. I've *got* to get back to camp, let them know I'm all right. You can see that, can't you?"

"Brazeau bridge? Camp?" He rubbed his left hand over his face. His voice was slurred. "No, you'd get lost in the forest."

"*You* got here, didn't you?"

"Yeah. An old man told me the way. Three days it took me, without food or water."

"Three days? You walked for three days with nothing to eat and drink? No wonder…" She stopped. She'd almost said: *No wonder you're out of your mind.*

"Sure. If you look for your spirit it's serious, you know. No food. No water. Seek with a pure heart, the Old One told me…" His voice trailed off into silence.

"The old man who told you the way?"

"Of course not. The old ones in the lodge…I *did* see them. They *did* talk to me. Told me to come north, find my grandmother." He was getting angry again, and Lenora tried to sit calmly, her hands folded in her lap, not letting him know how much he terrified her.

"I didn't know anyone lived out here."

"Downriver." He waved vaguely to the east. "Beautiful little lake. Used to catch brown trout there when I lived with Grandmother."

"There's a dam now. It's made a huge lake, like a hand. You don't mean there, do you?"

"Dam?" He stared at her dully.

Oh, boy, thought Lenora. *Now I've done it.* "How long since you were here with your grandmother?" she asked quickly.

"Ten, eleven years ago, maybe."

"You never went back?"

"My mom wouldn't let me. She said all that old stuff was no good. She said Grandmother had filled up my head with stories. She put me in school..." He stopped.

"Bad, huh?"

"Sometimes. There was one teacher in...in grade four, I think...used to read aloud to us. Man, that was interesting. Stories from all over the world, she said. Kind of like my grandmother's, but different. That was a good year."

"I'm just going into grade nine. It's kind of scary. In Alberta, junior high goes through grade nine — well, you know that, of course — so all the kids'll be friends already and I won't know *anyone.* It wouldn't have been so bad going into high school. I mean, it'd be new for everyone, wouldn't it?"

"I guess so." His voice was uninterested, but at least he didn't sound mad any more. He squatted on the sand not far from her, the axe held slackly in his right hand.

"What's your name?" she asked gently.

"Isaac. Isaac Manyfeathers."

"Aren't you lonely out here, in the forest?"

"Lonely?" Something sparked in his dull eyes. "Not here. Never here. I was lonely after I left Grandmother.

Mom...she was always out. Jobs or boy friends. You know. But it was worse in Calgary. Yeah, that was the worst."

"Worse than prison?" she dared to ask.

"Jail? That wasn't as bad as being on my own with no job and no friends. In jail I got a warm place to sleep and three meals a day. Only..."

"Yes?"

"Only the trees started talking to me, telling me I had to get away, go back to Grandmother's. I wanted to go so bad, but there were bars on the windows."

"So you escaped when you were out with a work party?"

"Did I? I guess I did. Yeah, that's right. I slept in the cemetery and found the medicine lodge. Yeah, that's right. And the old ones told me to come north to the river to look for my spirit. It was good being in the forest. Not lonely. Peaceful."

They sat silently for a while. Lenora glanced at his face. He was smiling, his eyes nearly closed. She moved cautiously and his eyes flew open.

"So you came to the river?" she asked, stretching her legs as if she were easing a cramp. Would she *ever* get away?

"I thought the spirit-seeking was over. The crows called me and I found you, right over there."

"Crows? I don't remember that at all. Guess I was really out of it."

"Red and white and yellow," he said suddenly. "Sun colours. And your hair, like the sun, drying by the fire. I thought I was someone real special, like in the old days, the sun child coming to *me*. But you're not the sun child, are you?" He was weeping, the tears running unheeded down his brown cheeks.

"I'm sorry. I'm afraid I'm not. I'm Lenora Rydz."

"But Thunderbird…I did see…no, that's wrong, too, isn't it? Not Thunderbird at all. No more spirit search. Nothing to hope for. To work for."

"Oh, please don't cry like that." Lenora was almost in tears herself. "There's always something to hope for."

"Like what?"

She shook her head. It was throbbing again and she felt a bit sick. "What are you going to do now?"

"Do?" He looked blank. "Guess I'll go to Grandmother's," he added after a moment's silence. "Yeah, there's still that."

"What about me? Isaac, it makes no sense to keep me here. Please let me go."

"You'll tell them where I am. They'll be after me."

"I won't. I swear I won't say a word. You go on to…to your grandmother's place. I'll wait here. The helicopter's bound to come back." Her voice wavered at the thought of the lonely vigil.

"No!" He brought his hands together. The axe blade glinted in a solitary beam of sunlight filtering through the dense trees. "You mustn't leave."

"All right," she said quickly. "Whatever you say." Her mind raced. Perhaps she could signal for help. But who would see her signal even if…?

The fire tower! In her mind she could hear Pete's quiet voice pointing out the different landmarks. The silver thread winding between the trees over to the north. *This* river. She had seen the river from the tower, so Pete would surely see her signal. How often did he make observations? What had he said when they said goodbye? "Every hour on the hour." That was it. But how early did he start his day? Would he be up now?

She looked cautiously at her watch. It was a bit before seven-thirty. Supposing that her watch was still keeping time after its dunking, in half an hour Pete would be at the top of his tower. She could signal in Morse code. A flashlight. Or a mirror. But she didn't have either. What could she *do*? She closed her eyes despairingly.

Smoke, she thought suddenly. *Stupid! That's what fire towers are for.* The one thing that would be sure to catch Pete's eye would be smoke. She had noticed, without really thinking about it, how carefully Isaac had tended the fire, using the driest of wood, so that it burned hot with no telltale smoke at all.

If she could get him to start a new fire…She shivered and hugged her arms across her chest. Isaac offered her his shirt, but she ignored him and knelt down at the place where the fire had been and began to gather together the charred fragments.

"I'm cold. You shouldn't have kicked the fire out.

"Let me. I'll fix it."

"Aren't you afraid the helicopter will come back again and see it?" She allowed a little scorn into her voice, not enough to make him really mad.

"Now that the sun is shining on the beach, he would never see it. Not the way I build a fire."

She watched him make a small hot fire. She sat close to it, her hands stretched out to it as if she were still cold, her eyes on the dial of her watch. The second hand swept around with feverish speed. The minutes ticked over. A quarter to eight. He sat opposite her, looking sombrely into the flames. She had to think of a way…

"I'm still hungry, and I can't eat the rest of that fish." She made her voice sulky. "It's disgusting. You kicked sand all over it."

"If I leave you here you'll try and run away."

"I won't. I promise."

"All right. I won't be long." He picked up the line and walked down to the river. As soon as his back was turned, she put two more logs on the fire.

Five minutes to eight. The logs were well alight, but the wood was seasoned and dry. There was no smoke at all. She got slowly to her feet. He was crouching on a rock in midstream, occupied in letting the fly drift downriver, pulling the line gently to bring it back. But he turned at once at her movement.

She waved. "Back in a minute," she called. She unzipped her shorts as she turned away, hoping that he would make the connection she intended and leave her alone. Once out of sight among the trees she zipped them up again and quickly began to tear up handfuls of dew-wet grass and to scoop up armfuls of damp aspen leaves.

Eight o'clock. From the shelter of a tree close to the water, she peered out. He was still intent on the fly drifting down on the current. She walked casually back to the fire, forcing herself to move without any urgency. Once at the fire she stood with her back to the water, so that her body masked the fire from him. Then she let the load of wet leaves and grass fall on the blazing logs.

At first she thought that she had overdone it and choked the fire to death. Then a cloud of dense white smoke suddenly rose. It was spectacular, far better than she had hoped. It was like a pillar of white on the still morning air. Her eyes began to water and she had to step back a pace.

If only she had something to signal with, she could try making the smoke go up in puffs. SOS. But it was probably trickier to do that it looked. If she were to smother the fire by mistake, she would have lost her only chance.

She stood perfectly still, watching the smoke, praying that Isaac might have hooked a fish, a giant, something splendid to occupy his whole attention. She prayed that Pete might not have picked this morning to sleep in. Perhaps his day didn't start till after eight. Maybe she'd blown her only chance by being too eager.

Go on, Pete, she urged him. Look to the north. *Look*. She could imagine him catching sight of the pillar of white smoke, taking a bearing on it, radioing the forest-warden station. She imagined it so clearly it became real. She could see him getting into his truck, bounding down the bumpy grass track to the road.

She was pushed to one side so abruptly that she lost her balance and fell. She lay on the sand watching Isaac's work boots kick and kick at the logs, as if they were an enemy. She lay quite still, her arms out in front of her. Her watch ticked on. Six minutes past eight.

12

Tuesday morning

"Why did you have to go and do that? I trusted you. Why did you do it?" He said the same words over and over. He was crying again, not caring that she could see the tears running down his brown cheeks. He had picked up the axe and his hand ran up and down the smooth, sweat-stained wood of the handle mechanically, as if he wasn't aware of what he was doing.

Lenora's eyes were fixed on the blade. *The axe! How could I forget it! I should have hidden it while he was fishing. Stupid! Stupid!*

She moistened her dry lips. "You can't blame me for trying to get away, Isaac," she said, trying to keep her voice low and reasonable, trying to make her body sit quietly by the ruined fire, when all it wanted to do was to get up and run screaming into the trees. "I just want to find my mom, tell her I'm all right. I wouldn't say anything about you…"

He wasn't paying attention. Her voice faded. He fumbled in the pockets of his shirt and she saw his face change. "My luck's gone."

"What's luck got to do with…?"

"My buffalo stone, that the old man told me to keep. He said it would bring me luck. It did, too. Brought me straight to the river. It was in the pocket of my shirt, that I covered you with yesterday…" His stare was hard.

"I didn't touch it, Isaac, honest. Maybe it fell out. It could be anywhere." She looked around helplessly at the sand-and-shingle beach. "You'll never find it here. I'm sorry."

"My luck's gone," he said again. "It's all been for nothing, hasn't it? Never found my spirit. You don't think I'm going to find my grandmother in her old place, do you? I heard what you said about them building a dam."

"I don't know. Maybe I've got it wrong. Or maybe she's gone to live on the reserve. You might find her there."

"I stayed away too long. I should have come back to see her. Now it's too late. If she's gone it's no good. Running away. Just plain stupid."

"It was an impulse, Isaac, that's all. Give yourself up and explain to them how you feel, how you had to see your grandmother, how the trees called you…" Her voice faded as he shook his head.

"And have them put me in the Alberta hospital? I'm not *that* crazy. No, I'm not going back. If I do, they'll send me back to that other place, where I'll be locked up all day and never see trees and sky. You don't know how bad it can be in places like that, Lenora. Men act like animals when they're penned up together. Worse than animals."

"Maybe your grandmother is still there. Maybe not. But if she isn't, what do you plan to do then? Go back to your mom?"

He shook his head. "The police are sure to go to Mom's, first thing they'd do, I guess. What'll I do? I'll stay here. Yeah, that's what I'll do. And you, too. If you stay, nobody'll ever know I'm here. They'll never find us. We won't starve, you don't have to be scared of that. There's roots and berries. And plenty of fish. You liked the fish, didn't you?''

Lenora tried to push down her rising panic and argue rationally. "Isaac, you just haven't thought it out. What about winter? It's chilly enough at night now and it's still August. In another month there'll be frost, maybe snow. There's no way we could survive up here without winter clothing and shelter, is there?''

He said nothing, just looked obstinate, and she went on. "Anyway, like I said, all you've done so far is run away from a work party. That was a dumb thing to do, but it didn't hurt anybody. But if you don't let me go, if you make me stay, Mom and my stepfather are going to hunt for me. There'll be an organized search with helicopters and hundreds of people, the army and police and all. You wouldn't stand a chance of getting away from them. Then, when they've found us and they know you've kept me against my will, well, that's kidnapping, and I don't know what the penalty for that is, but I bet it's *years*.''

"You could tell them you stayed with me of your own free will, couldn't you?''

"Oh, Isaac!" Lenora was torn between tears and laughter.

"You *said* you were lonely, too. You *said* you were scared of having to go to a new school. You said you didn't have any friends. Be my friend and stay. Please.''

Lenora bit her lip. Why had she shared her feelings of loneliness with this strange boy? She hadn't even told Mom exactly how she felt. She had just been talking, babbling anything that came into her head, anything to distract him from his anger, from the axe in his hand. Maybe she saw in his anger and pain something she shared, in however small a measure. In a small way, she did feel close to his loneliness and loss of roots.

Boy, that doesn't say much for Mom and your com- fortable life, does it? a cynical voice sneered inside her.

No, I'm not being fair. Mom's okay. Better than okay, sometimes. But... She struggled with the bitter concept. *Maybe all of us are alone most of the time. Each one in his or her own prison. No matter how hard you try, you can't really share your thoughts, the things that matter most. Except with a few special people, like Dad. But most of the time there just don't seem to be words that fit how a person feels. Maybe life is really about understanding this prison and trying to break free of it, any way you can. I suppose believing in God would be the best way. Being a great artist or a poet like Dad would help. But I'll never be that. I'm too dumb. Maybe just reaching out to someone else who's trying to get free would do.*

She pulled her thoughts back to Isaac, who was talk- ing again. "...the forest is a good place to be, honest. It doesn't cheat you the way people do."

He was looking at her expectantly, waiting for her answer. "Be my friend, and stay," he had said. What was she to do? What could she say?

"Isaac, I'd like to be your friend, truly. But being your friend can't mean giving up my life, the way it's supposed to be for me. I can't run away from school just because I'm scared to death that I'll never make friends and they'll despise me and I'll be behind with the work and I'll have to qualify all over again for the swimming team. Because going to school is what I'm supposed to do right now."

"What about me? What am *I* supposed to do!"

"You know that as well as I do."

"I can't give myself up. I won't go back there. It isn't fair. I didn't do anything, except be an idiot."

"What did...I mean, would you like to tell me about it? Maybe it would help. The forestry warden didn't say much — just something about breaking into a warehouse."

"Ben and Moses and Jim did that. I didn't even know about it till it was over."

"Were they friends of yours?"

"I thought they were. We got together at the Calgary bus depot. I hadn't had any work in weeks and I was bumming, looking for a handout, enough for the bus ride as far as Red Deer. I was thinking then that I'd go look for Grandmother."

"You didn't try hitching?"

"I'd thumbed a ride down from Edmonton the year before with no trouble at all. But I sure couldn't pick up a ride back. Couldn't figure it out till I went into the washroom at the bus depot and saw myself in the mirror there. Well, I'd been living on the streets pretty well for weeks. I was a mess. I guess I wouldn't have given myself a ride."

"So these guys just picked you up at the bus depot? I wonder what they were doing there. I mean do you think meeting you was just coincidence?"

Isaac shook his head. "Never thought about it at the time, but now...I guess they were cruising around looking for a mug. And they found one." He laughed bitterly.

"Don't be hard on yourself. For all you know, they were experts."

"I didn't think. I was just so grateful. They gave me food and beer and promised me a place to stay. You just don't know what that meant to me right then. They even said they'd try and help me find some work. I..."

"Go on."

"I knew they weren't up to much, Lenora. But a big city's an awful place to be alone with no job, no money, no friends. I guess I just shut my eyes to what they were and went along with them."

"So how did you finish up at that warehouse?"

"They said we were going to a party and they pushed me into this truck — Moses and Ben, that was. Jim went off by himself. They drove around and parked in a laneway. It was dark by then, I couldn't see a thing. Then they got out and told me to wait for them, said they'd be back in a minute.

"I was so dumb! I sat there, getting more and more nervous, just feeling something was wrong, but not having any idea what it was. Wanting to get the heck out of there, but not wanting to leave my new friends in the lurch." He gave a bitter laugh.

"Friends! Next thing I know there's a blinding light in my eyes. I just make out a car at the end of the lane. When I look over my shoulder there's a car at the other end. Even then I don't know what's going on. Not till a couple of cops drag me out of the truck." He rubbed his hand over his face.

"Jeez. After that it was kind of like a bad dream. All mixed up and me not making sense out of it. I'm shoved in a police car and I'm on my way to jail, still not knowing exactly what's going on, but getting the idea that the truck's stolen."

"What about the others?"

"Got clean away. It wasn't till my trial I found out what had happened. The warehouse I was parked behind was full of stereo stuff, and they must have triggered the alarm system, breaking in. They grabbed what they could and took off. The cops said there must have been a second truck. Jim would have been driving it. He must have picked it up after he left us and he was waiting for the others. Yeah, they grabbed the stuff and ran, leaving me sitting in a stolen truck for the police to pick up."

"Didn't you tell them?"

"What was there to tell? I didn't even know where

they lived — they'd picked me up at the bus depot and taken me to a bar. But even if I could have helped them, I wouldn't. They'd been my friends, buying me beer and something to eat."

"Isaac! They set you up. What you need are some real friends. And a good lawyer."

"I've got no money for lawyers. What'd be the use anyway? I escaped from jail. That's a black mark against me. They'd never listen now."

"Yes, they would. They *will*. I'll ask my stepfather to help you. He'll know exactly how to get hold of the right kind of lawyer. I don't know how much it'll cost, but we'll manage. I'll pay him back. Don't worry. Harry'll know just what to do."

With a rush of thankfulness, Lenora realized that indeed Harry *could* be counted on to do something to help, once it had been explained to him properly. How comfortable it was, how safe it felt to have someone in the family you could really trust to help you, when help was needed.

My goodness, that must be exactly how Mom feels, she realized. *That's really why she fell in love with Harry. She needs someone to rely on. And I'll bet that Harry married her because he needs someone to look after, now that his boys are growing up. They are made for each other. Why did I never see that before? How could I have been so dumb?*

Harry was trustworthy. Denis had made that clear when he'd explained how his dad had brought up the two boys single-handedly. And she could guess that once he'd made up his mind about something, like an injustice being done, he'd never turn back from it, no matter how tough it might be to fix. Only explaining it to him properly, so he'd understand and be on their side, that was going to be the catch;

because if ever there was a person as pig-headed and obstinate and set in his ways as Harry Mathieson, she hadn't met him.

She sighed, It wasn't going to be easy. If only Dad were here. She had always been able to talk to Dad, and he had always understood what she meant, even if she couldn't put it into words properly. Maybe it was because he was Polish and a poet and that made him particularly sensitive and understanding.

Then she tried to imagine what Dad would actually *do* in this case. She knew he'd understand and really empathize with her feelings and with poor Isaac. He'd comfort her and make her feel better. Then maybe he'd retire to his study and write a bitter poem about the injustices of the penal system in Canada. But she had to admit that he wouldn't have the slightest idea of where to find a good criminal lawyer or how you went about appealing a conviction.

Thinking like this made her feel a traitor, and she pushed the thoughts out of her head and concentrated on sending him a powerful message of love, all the way across the prairies to Toronto. Then she looked up, to see Isaac's dark eyes fastened on her. *I do love you, Dad. I always will. But...*

"Yes, you can really trust Harry," she said confidently. "What we've got to do is to work out exactly what to tell him so that he understands. I mean, it's no good talking about sun dances and spirit searches and stuff like that. They're yours, anyway. Private and no one else's business. And they'd just muddle Harry."

"But it was the trees talking to me and the old medicine lodge and..."

"Listen, Isaac. You ran away from the work party on impulse, that's all, and headed north to your grandmother's place. Why did you want to go there?"

"I thought she'd help me. Straighten out my head."

"Tell them exactly that. So you escaped and got as far as the river, and then you found me. Where? You never did tell me what happened."

"You were washed up on that sandbar over there. Half in the river. You were unconscious and cold, like ice. It didn't make sense, if you were the sun child…" Isaac stopped and shook his head, confused for a second.

"No, forget that. It didn't really happen, only in your head. You came along and dragged me ashore and got me warmed up. If you hadn't done all the right things I'd have died, wouldn't I? You stopped running away and looked after me. Don't you see how important that's going to be, Isaac? You stopped and saved my life. Oh, my goodness, you really *did*. And I never even thanked you. Isaac, I'm sorry."

"That's all right," he muttered. "I don't think I'd have done it if I hadn't been a bit crazy. I thought you were sent to me, that I was something special. The way you looked and the colours of your clothes, sun colours. I thought…"

"No, Isaac. Forget your sun child dream. Maybe you *were* a bit out of your mind with not eating and drinking all that time. But you can't tell how you'd have behaved if you had been okay. The important thing is that you *did* stop and save my life. I know I'm not anyone special or important, but don't you see? They're bound to take it into account when you give yourself up."

"No!" He was on his feet, his knuckles white around the handle of the axe. "No, I'm not going to listen to you anymore. You're not going to talk me into going back to prison just because we're friends. No way."

He turned and began to run downstream along the river's edge, leaping from shingle beach to sandbar and back, taking a shortcut across the big curve of the river.

"Please wait." She ran after him. "Isaac, please. You'll ruin everything if you run now. Trust me. And Harry. He'll help you, I swear."

Isaac paused for a second, then went on. She stood at the edge of the river, the cold water frothing around her ankles. *Oh, Isaac. If only you'd trust me. But why should you? What have we ever done that you should trust us anyway?*

There was a rustling among the trees close to where the fire had been. She turned. *It's Pete,* she thought. *Oh, thank God! He's seen my fire and come along one of the fire cuts in his truck.*

"I'm here," she yelled. "Down by the river." She got back to the shore and began to run towards the sound.

It was very loud now. More than one person. More like a herd of elephants. She stopped. Backed up a step, suddenly afraid.

Out of the scatter of aspen and berry bushes that edged the river bank came a huge, dark, lumbering shape. She screamed till her throat hurt. It stopped, rearing up on its hind legs, as tall as a man, its head weaving to and fro, sniffing the air. Its tiny eyes were barely visible in the thick brown fur. *Maybe it won't see me.* She stopped screaming and stood still, her hand stuffed in her mouth, biting down on the knuckles. *Only a black bear,* she told herself. But it looked enormous standing there on the bank above her. Quite different from the ones in the Toronto zoo.

The bear flopped forward onto all fours and moved towards her. It slid down the bank and encountered their camp. Its nose went down. It searched among the scattered ashes of the fire. Its muzzle must have touched a still-hot ember, and it let out an almost human yelp; but it went on pawing at the ground, its big head weaving from side to side. She could hear slurping noises, as the bear devoured the head and insides of the fish Isaac had buried.

Slowly Lenora backed away. She stumbled and felt wet shingle under her hands. Her fingers folded around a big stone. Then she let it go. What was the use? She tried to get to her feet again, but her knees seemed to have turned to rubber. Sweat started out on her forehead and the bear's nose came up.

Animals can smell fear, she remembered. She told her body not to be afraid. Again the bear reared up hugely on its hind legs. It stood still, its head weaving almost blindly to and fro, sniffing her fear. It looked at the same time stupid and terrifying.

In spite of herself, a scream tore out of her throat. The bear seemed to make up its mind. It dropped to all fours and began to lumber towards her, not charging, but at a steady trot.

She had time to notice the funny way its fat paws toed in as it came. Time to see the claws like miniature scythes, five to a paw. She couldn't run away. She couldn't move her legs at all. She crouched with hands folded over the back of her head and waited for the slashing attack. She had time to wonder how much it would hurt and what it would feel like to be dead.

Time stopped. She could smell its strong scent. Then she heard the sound of something whistling through the air. A dull thunk and a hideous roar, like the voices of all the monsters of a nightmare rolled into one. She shut her eyes tighter and crouched low to the ground.

"Lenora, get up. Run!" Isaac's voice yelled from behind her.

She opened her eyes. Directly in her path the bear lay on its side, it legs stuck out stiffly in front of it.

Blood bubbled thickly from its neck. She managed to get to her feet, to take a stiff step back towards Isaac. Away from the yellow teeth bared in a snarl, the claws like curved swords. There was a horrible moaning sound, like an animal's. She was making it. She didn't know how to stop it. Or the shaking.

She saw the axe, its blade buried deep in the bear's neck, the fur dark and sticky around it. *Oh, Isaac, you saved my life again.*

She turned away from the horror at her feet, turned to run back to Isaac. He was standing with his hands hanging at his sides. It was the first time she'd seen him without his axe, except when he'd lain it down to fish. He looked different.

At that moment, from the bush behind her, came the sound of familiar voices calling her name, voices from the safe, comfortable past that had nothing to do with this mythic world of sun dances and axes and bears. She stopped.

"Lenora, are you there? Lenora!"

She turned her back on Isaac. There they were, breaking out of the trees only about fifty metres from the fire. Harry and Peter and....

She began to run. "Denis, you're alive! I thought maybe...I'm so glad..."

She ran uncaringly past the great bulk of fur and muscle and bones. Around the bear's glistening muzzle, the flies were already starting to buzz.

Denis jumped down onto the beach and ran to meet her. He gave her a rib-cracking hug. "I thought you were dead, too. I've been feeling like a murderer ever since yesterday. Jeez, I was never so glad of anything in my life as to hear you screeching." His voice was teasing as if he'd been her brother forever, and she fell happily into the same pattern of banter.

"Screeching? Well, I guess you'd have screeched if you'd had a dirty great bear after you. What *took* you so long?"

"A bear? You're kidding" He walked past her and stopped. "Hey, who's that?"

Lenora turned again. Isaac was still standing alone on the beach. He hadn't moved. Without the familiar axe, he looked much younger, more vulnerable. Spent. As if he might drop at any moment. What had gone into that mighty throw that had sent the axe blade slicing through the heavy muscle of the bear's neck to sever the main artery?

She stood close to the fire, wanting to run to him, to show him that she was on his side. But somehow she couldn't move. She just stood, her position mirroring his, her hands limp at her sides.

Then Pete pushed past her and walked along the beach. Isaac didn't move. He just stood staring at Lenora. Pete put a hand on his shoulder and spoke to him. He flinched and she saw his body sag. He didn't look like the boy who had terrified her. He didn't look like her friend Isaac. He was just a native boy with sullen features and dirty prison clothes.

They were walking up the beach towards her now, Pete and his prisoner. She took a step forward, but he didn't look at her. Just walked right past as if she wasn't there.

She could feel tears prick at her eyes and she looked away, down at the beach. There were the remnants of her signal fire. The spurts of sand where Isaac's angry feet had kicked it out. The bear's raking claw marks... What was that, close to the embers? Like a huge snail. She bent and picked it up, turning it over in her hand. It wasn't a shell, but a stone, a fossil shell. Isaac's luck.

Maybe he'll feel better when I give it back to him, she thought. *But not now. If I gave it him now he'd only throw it away. I'll wait until he's forgiven me for not being the sun child he needed, for turning away from him to my family, for just being Lenora Rydz.*

13

October

Isaac hesitated. "In you go." The guard's voice came from behind him and he pushed open the door.

Lenora was sitting on the visitor's side of the room. She was wearing a cherry-red coat with a beret to match, and her hair, bright as sunshine, spread over her shoulders. He stood staring, wanting to stretch out his hands to its warmth.

She smiled a small nervous smile. "They said I could talk to you just the once, for ten minutes."

He sat down then. "You okay?"

"I'm fine."

"How did school turn out?"

Her eyes looked larger than ever and he saw she was close to tears. "You actually remembered how I was dreading it! It turned out okay, much better than I expected."

"I'm glad."

"What about you? Are you okay?"

He glanced around the green-painted room and shrugged. "I guess."

She looked down at her fingers, twisting them together. "Isaac, do you forgive me? That last morning. I'm sorry."

"Forgive?" He pretended to misunderstand.

She looked up and his eyes followed hers to the large wall clock. "There's so little time. That last morning, down by the river, we were telling the truth to each other, becoming real friends. Then you saved my life for the second time. But instead of standing by you I ran to my family, to Denis."

"It was the natural thing to do, I guess."

"I know it was natural. That's what I mean. If I'd have thought…"

"Then you'd have stood by me? But it'd have just been a kind of play-acting, wouldn't it?"

"I suppose, but…"

"Sure, it hurt at the time to see you turn your back on me. But I don't know if it would have made any difference if you *had* turned to me instead of your stepbrother there. I mean, when that warden came out of the trees I knew it was the end of my dream. I was hurting so much inside I don't suppose anything you could have done would have made a difference."

"But…"

"Lenora, it doesn't bother me now. You've just got to forgive yourself, and then there'll be nothing in the way of our being friends — except maybe your family not wanting you to associate with a jailbird." He managed a bitter grin.

"That's okay." Her smile was so radiant he blinked. "It was Harry who fixed it so I could see you today. Harry's been marvellous. And of course Mom would do anything for you after she found out you'd saved my life — twice! So that's all right. All you've got to do is to hang on. The lawyers are working on your case. Just promise you won't give up. That you'll follow your spirit."

"Spirit? What I did was pretty crazy."

"Hermits used to go off alone, all the time, not eating or drinking. They heard voices and saw visions, too."

"What's that prove?" He couldn't help grinning at the idea of him being like a holy man. "That they were crazy, too?"

"Maybe turning off the sounds of the world the way you did made you a bit crazy. But you had to turn them off to hear what was really going on inside your head, didn't you?"

He nodded. "That's true. And for a while it all seemed so simple, when I was off my head and thought you were the sun child. It's not that clear any more. It's harder now. I think that then I was running away from reality, not just from the world noise. I was running away right up to that moment when I killed the bear."

She shivered and folded her arms across her chest as if she were cold in spite of her woollen coat. "What was it like then?"

"Like the end of a dream," he said slowly. "When I saw the bear lumbering across the beach towards you, I knew who he was. 'Hey, spirit,' I said to myself. 'You took a long time getting here.' And I watched him get closer, kind of in a trance. Then it was like the earth shook, just for a second. And afterwards everything around me looked different: the sky, the trees, the bear coming towards you and you crouching on the ground. And there wasn't any time for thinking. My arm and shoulder just did what they had to do."

"It was a fabulous throw, Isaac."

"Yeah." He sat tall.

"So you *did* find your spirit! But you had to kill it. Didn't you feel just awful about that?"

He shook his head. "At the time I was just numb. Like I'd killed myself. But I worked it all out later, in jail. I've been doing a lot of thinking in here. Sure I had to kill the bear's body. But my axe couldn't touch its spirit, you see? And I think killing it got rid of the dreaming part of me that was still stuck back in Grandmother's house, the part of me that kept getting in the way of Mom and school and everything else that happened to me."

"Your grandmother's house…Did Harry tell you…?"

"About the dam. Kind of funny, isn't it? All those years I was dreaming about the place I wanted to be, the place where I thought I belonged, it wasn't there. It was under water."

"He couldn't find your grandmother. I'm awfully sorry."

"Yeah. It's too bad. I guess *her* dream was a bit stronger than reality, too. That's why Mom took me away from her, because she wouldn't move. She'd have had me stay with her, not believing that the water would ever come and fill the whole valley." He sighed. "Sometimes I feel closer to Grandmother than anyone."

"Like me and Dad. And it got in the way of getting to know Harry and understanding Mom's feelings. All the emotions damming up the current, like the log jam, I guess. Don't let what happened to your grandmother stop you from working things out."

"Don't worry. My head may spin in the sun dance once in a while, but I've got my feet firmly on the ground, like Old Bear's."

"I'm glad, Isaac."

"It's you did it for me, and Mr. Mathieson. He's promised that if I finish high school through correspondence he'll help me get training and a career in forestry."

"He told me. You'll be back with your beloved trees. Have you seen your mom yet?"

"No." He rubbed his hands over his face. "I'm still working on that. I do know that taking me to Edmonton was the best thing she could think of back then. I've just got to do a bit more thinking about it before I talk to her. I want to be fair, see. Start off clean with no hard feelings."

"I've got to go. Isaac, I wanted to tell you I've got your lucky stone. I wanted to give it to you, but they wouldn't let me. I promise I'll keep it safe and give it back the day you get out."

"My lucky stone!" He held out a cupped hand. He could almost see it, like a huge stone snail, curled in the hollow of his palm. "Buffalo stone, the old man called it."

"Brian says it's an ammonite. That's the fossil of a shellfish that lived maybe a hundred million years ago, when Alberta was all sea. Long before people."

"My lucky stone, that I kicked out of the ground? Before my people?"

"Before any human beings. Before there was land here."

"Makes our kind of time look silly, doesn't it?" Isaac looked at the clock. The hands whizzed by. She'd be gone in a minute, taking the light with her. He knew that time would slow down as soon as she'd left. Time ahead looked pretty grey.

He'd better keep his mind fixed on his lucky stone. A hundred million years. A few months in jail wasn't much when you thought of time that way. That was the way to look at Grandmother's stories, too. Not as a going back. Not as "if only things were different"... but as part of the pattern of going forward.

One day his spirit search and the killing of the bear would make a story, like her stories, for *his* grandchildren and great-grandchildren. So he'd better make sure that his story came out the way he'd want them to hear it...

The outer door was unlocked. Lenora was standing and he got to his feet, too.

"Goodbye." Tears rolled out of her eyes and she brushed them away angrily and busied herself with pulling on her red woolly gloves.

"I'll see you," he said boldly and went out quickly, so he could hold the colours of her coat and hair in his mind's eye.

Harry was waiting for her. He tucked her arm through his as they walked across the parking lot.

"All right, Lenora?"

"Yes, thanks, Harry. I mean, *really* thanks. For helping Isaac and understanding how I felt."

He laughed wryly. "Helping Isaac's been the easy part. Understanding you... well, according to Hazel, that'll probably take the rest of my life."

"I don't *mean* to be difficult."

"Perhaps challenging would be a better description, eh?"

As he spoke, Lenora realized that Harry intended to apply to *her* the same energy that he'd put into the army, to his second career, and to bringing up the boys. Probably that he'd bring to his and Mom's marriage.

A giggle rose in her throat and threatened to explode. *Heaven help us both,* she thought. Then she got serious. For difficult though life with the new Harry might be, she understood that he was going to tackle it because he really cared for Hazel and her. And it was going to be up to her to do her part to make it work. Her fingers felt the coiled ammonite in her pocket.